D1713700

JUST BENEATH
MY SKIN

DARREN GREER

Cormorant Books

Canada Council   Conseil des Arts
for the Arts   du Canada

The publisher gratefully acknowledges the support of the Canada Council for the
Arts and the Ontario Arts Council for its publishing program. We acknowledge
the financial support of the Government of Canada through the Canada Book
Fund (CBF) for our publishing activities, and the Government of Ontario through
the Ontario Media Development Corporation, an agency of the Ontario Ministry
of Culture, and the Ontario Book Publishing Tax Credit Program.

LIBRARY AND ARCHIVES CANADA CATALOGUING IN PUBLICATION

Greer, Darren
Just beneath my skin / Darren Greer.

Issued also in electronic formats.
ISBN 978-1-77086-255-5

1. Title.

PS8563.R4315J88 2013   C813'.6   C2013-900472-6

Cover photo and design: Angel Guerra/Archetype
Interior text design: Tannice Goddard, Soul Oasis Networking
Printer: Friesens

Printed and bound in Canada.

The interior of this book is printed on 100% post-consumer waste recycled paper.

CORMORANT BOOKS INC.
10 ST. MARY STREET, SUITE 615, TORONTO, ONTARIO, M4Y 1P9
www.cormorantbooks.com

For Scott

Who was your father, Jewel?
   — *As I Lay Dying*, William Faulkner

My doom has come upon me; let me not then die
ingloriously and without a struggle, but let me first
do some great thing that shall be told among men
hereafter.
   — *The Iliad of Homer*, Samuel Butler, (translator)

Part I

IT'S RAINING WHEN I SEE Jake outside Douglas's store passing around a bottle of wine with Charlie Whynot and Johnny Lang. They're standing under the awning. You can see ol' Douglas through the window behind the counter, pointing and waving at them to go away. They won't. They just stand there making it hard for customers to get by.

I stand on the other side of the street and stare at them, 'cause I haven't seen Jake since he left for Halifax. He doesn't see me at first, until Johnny Lang points me out. Jake hollers for me to come over. I do, but I don't go under the awning. I stand on the sidewalk holding the carton of milk Mom sent me to the store to get for her tea and say, "Hiya Jake."

"Heyya squirt," Jake says. "You look like a drowned rat."

"He is a rat," says Johnny, scowling at me as he takes the bottle from Jake. "His mother is, so I don't see why he wouldn't be."

"Ahh, leave it," says Jake to Johnny. "What you up to, squirt?"

"I thought you were still in Halifax," I say.

Jake shrugs. "I'm home for a bit."

"For good?" I ask him.

"For a visit," says Jake.

3

"Jake's back!" cackles Charlie Whynot when it's his turn for the wine. "Oh yes he is!"

Charlie is my mom's cousin. She says he's crazy as two barrels of monkey shit. He wears one white cotton glove on his left hand and nothing on his right because he's a fan of Michael Jackson. Sometimes he wears mirrored sunglasses. He knows how to moonwalk. Last year he tried to home perm his hair into tight little curls like Michael Jackson's, though it didn't work. His hair is light brown and straight as a board. It came out all fluffy with big floppy curls like a girl's. Everybody said he looked like a faggot and wondered what a white man was doing taking after a nigger. "'Cause," was Charlie's answer. "That nigger makes more money in one day than this whole shitty little town will ever make put together in their entire lives. That's fucking why." After the perm wore off he didn't try to curl his hair anymore, though he still wears one white glove and listens to the *Thriller* album at least once a day and moonwalks on the sidewalk downtown sometimes and doesn't care who's watching. He's crazy all right, but compared to Johnny Lang, who he hangs around, he's okay.

"Jake's back, and he brought us this." Charlie holds up the bottle in his white-gloved hand. "Jake's got money. Jake's rich, ain't ya, old Jakey! Jake's gonna take care of his friends, ain't ya, bub!" Jake shrugs and reaches for the bottle.

"Is that right, Jake?" I say. "Are you rich?"

Jake looks at me. The rain's falling harder now and I'm starting to shiver. He takes me by the shoulder and pulls me in under the awning.

"Why aren't you in school?" he says.

"No school today," I say. "It's Saturday. No school yesterday either. Teacher's marking day."

4

"It's September," says Jake, "and already the teachers take a marking day?"

"Fucking teachers," says Johnny. He spits on the steps. "Someone should gut 'em with a knife and leave 'em to bleed all over their fucking exams."

We all look at Johnny. You never know when he says things like that whether he means it. But he only snatches the bottle away from Jake and says, "What you morons lookin' at?" and takes another swig. Jake turns to me and says he thinks it's time I go home.

"Are ya coming over, Jake? Mom will be glad to see ya."

"Maybe," Jake says. "You tell her you saw me?"

"If you want me to."

"Well, then … tell her I'll drop around tonight and that when I do I want to talk to her."

"Okay, Jake. I will. What do you want to talk to Mom about?"

"None of your business," Jake says. "Now git."

I don't. Douglas starts waving through the window again at Jake and his friends to go away. "Hold your horses, old man," Johnny says, as if Douglas can hear through the glass. Thick glass. Double-paned. I know because Halloween last year someone threw a rock and Douglas raised ol' hell 'cause it cost him a hundred dollars to replace. "McNeil," Johnny says. "You gonna buy us more White Shark, or do we gotta beat it out of you?"

"I'll buy it," Jake says. "Should we send Charlie?"

"The rain's lettin' up. Let's all go. We can go back to my place and get shit-faced."

They zip up their jackets and get ready to leave. "Beat it, shit-for-brains," Johnny Lang says, giving me a push out from underneath the awning. I look at Jake.

"Johnny's right," he says. "Go home."

"But Jake ..."

"Go home!" Jake orders. And then, "Don't worry. I'll see you tonight."

I stand there and watch 'em cross the road. They head down Main Street towards the Nova Scotia Liquor Commission, all three in black leather jackets with shoulders hunched against the rain.

Cold, black, day-after-marking-day rain.

DRIVING FROM HALIFAX DOWN TO North River, pushing the Pinto as hard as she would go and playing Houses of the Holy in the tape deck, I remembered something my old man used to say. The river flows only one way. I was never sure what he meant by that, other than to say that you can't go back in time, but doesn't everyone already know that?

Then again, my father is a master of the obvious. He used to say a lot of things I never agreed with. But this one kept coming back to me. The river flows only one way, the river flows only one way, the river flows only one way.

What river? The Memragouche? He never said, but that must have been the river he meant, because there aren't any other rivers in North River. I remember the stories my granddad used to tell me about it, stories my father never had much time for. He always said my grandfather was an uneducated, ungodly fool of a man with barely two teeth in his head and a too-simple heart. This was another of my father's sayings that bothered me, for as true as all these things about my grandfather seemed to be, they were also the things I liked most about him when I was a kid. It was true, for instance, that he had no teeth. When my father would take me to visit him he would wait until my old man's back was turned and thrust his top dentures out of his mouth with his tongue and let them fall into his lap. Then he would look at me with his mouth collapsed in on itself and all wormy and smile, and I would giggle behind my hands. By the time my father turned around, Granddad McNeil's dentures would be back in, and we would be sitting innocent as pie, him drinking his tea and me the chocolate milk Nana McNeil made for me out of fresh cow's milk, powdered cocoa and a tablespoon of sugar.

In between he'd tell me about the loggers, and how they would drive herds of cut trees down the river from the Memragouche lakes to the match and lumber mills below Great Falls. Men would ride and roll the logs, he told me, poling and prodding the ones that hung up on the banks or that slowed and gathered in creases in the eddies. It was a dangerous job. Men slipped and got crushed between two logs just as they were being tossed together on the currents, or drowned when they went all the way under and never got a break in the logs to come back up again. My grandfather was one of the lucky ones. He rode the logs for years and never got so much as a soaker.

My grandfather's dead now, and the river logging stopped years ago. There's boom trucks to bring in the pulp logs these days. I would lie in my room nights when I was a kid after my granddad talked to me and I'd imagine I could hear the men shouting on the river outside my window, the thunder of the logs as they crashed together, the squeaking of the herd, stripped of their bark, rubbing against each other as they floated gently by. I heard this so clear in my mind that one time I asked my father if it couldn't have been ghosts I was hearing on the river at night. I was only twelve.

"Could be, Jacob," said my father. "I've heard of stranger things happening under the Lord's blue sky."

Like most ministers, and all Baptists, my father believed everything invisible was a possibility.

And everything real was a sin.

THE ROAD FOLLOWS THE RIVER. Jake used to tell me that once there were loggers on the river and a bunch of mills and Indians in canoes. It's hard to believe now 'cause it's just a river, and in the summer below the mill it stinks of sulphur and foam clings to the banks as thick and yellow as pus. But up here it's okay. Mom lets me go swimming off the bank where Harmony Lake Road meets Highway #7. There aren't any other kids on Harmony Lake Road. Last year Wendy McNutt had a baby girl called Lucy but she died right after. Wendy came crying and screaming down the road in the middle of the night in her nightdress when she found her. Our neighbour, Irene Lang, took her in and called the police and got her calmed some. Mom said the baby died of crib death. I didn't know what this meant 'til Jake told me that sometimes babies die for no good reason.

"So why do they call it crib death?"

"'Cause they just die in their cribs," Jake said, "and that's where their mother finds them."

I asked Jake if older kids could die like that too. Jake laughed and said as far as he knew it was just babies. Still, I tried to stay awake for a few nights after in case I just stopped breathing and

Mom came in and found me all blue and cold in my bed in the morning.

That's how they found Lucy. Blue and cold. I heard Irene telling Mom the day after it happened. "As blue and cold as a fish," said Irene. "I swear she was. Poor thing must have been dead for hours."

A few times after I dreamed baby Lucy was in bed with me, blue like Irene said. Her eyes were open and looking at me and she was frowning. I woke up scared in the dark and couldn't sleep again 'til morning. I kept falling asleep in Mrs. Burns's Grade Two class all that week until she called Mom and told her I wasn't getting enough rest. Mom yelled at me for staying awake reading *Archie Digest*. I didn't tell her about baby Lucy. I didn't want anyone to know.

I WOULD HAVE GONE RIGHT out to Carla's and seen Nathan as soon as I got into North River, except I drove past Johnny Lang and Charlie Whynot hanging out in the liquor store parking lot on my way through town. I could have driven by and pretended I didn't see them, but you don't play those games with Johnny Lang. I've known him since we were in school together, and I've always managed to stay on the right side of him. But that could change. I'd seen it. Guys who he'd never had a beef with, he'd suddenly decide he didn't like anymore. When that happened, watch the fuck out. So when Johnny waved me down from the parking lot I turned in to see what he wanted. As soon as I did they jumped in without asking. Charlie in back and Johnny in front.

"Hey Jake," said Charlie. I noticed he was still wearing that stupid fucking white glove.

"Heyya fuckface," said Johnny. "I thought you got smart and left this shithole for good."

"I did," I told him. "I'm just home to see Carla and the kid."

"That bitch," said Johnny. "You give me the word, man, and I'll take care of her. You can take the kid to the city and never bring him back, for all I care."

"Naw," I said. "It's okay. I got my own methods."

Johnny shrugged. "Whatever."

I wouldn't put it past Johnny to waste Carla if I asked him. Not because he's devoted to me or anything, but because Johnny's just itching to waste somebody, and it would be better if he had a good reason. Once I heard he beat up some guy from Oldsport in his cabin up on River Road and nearly killed him. I don't know what the fight was about, but Johnny was having a party, and Johnny's parties usually ended with him beating up some guy from Oldsport. Someone called the cops, and by the time they got there they found everyone cleared out, the guy unconscious in the middle of the living-room floor, and Johnny and Charlie kneeling beside him trying to start Johnny's Husqvarna power saw. Fortunately for the guy, whoever he was, Johnny had flooded it, and when the RCMP officer asked him what he thought he was doing, Johnny supposedly said, "What the fuck does it look like I'm doing? Having a tea party?"

They arrested him and he spent a few nights in jail. But the guy wouldn't lay charges and they could never prove Johnny wasn't seriously intent on just cutting up some wood for his stove with the power saw. I asked him once, when we were drunk and I worked up the nerve, if he would really have cut the guy up into little pieces.

"Do birds fucking fly, McNeil?" he said, and he asked me to pass the bottle.

Johnny Lang is seriously disturbed, and it makes me nervous just to be around him. But as my dad is fond of saying, you make your bed, you lie in it. I made my bed with Johnny long ago, probably from the first day I met him in high school. He gave me a pack of smokes that day, I remember. I was broke, and I'd asked him for one smoke, and he took an extra pack out of his jacket and gave me the whole thing. He can be really generous

13

to people he likes, and really dangerous to those he doesn't. The scariest thing about him is how easily you can fall from one category into the other. The thing with Johnny is you are either a friend or an enemy: there is no in-between.

Being either is dangerous.

MOM IS SITTING AT THE kitchen table like she was when I left. She has a cup of tea beside her and the *Oldsport Banner* open on her lap. "It's about time," she says. "I needed that milk for my tea a half hour ago."

"I'm sorry," I say. "I —"

"Never mind. Bring it here."

I do. She opens the carton, pours a dash into her cup, and gives it back and tells me to put it in the fridge. When I turn around again she's gone back to the *Banner*. I don't know how to tell her about Jake so I just stand there until she looks up again.

"What the blazes is wrong with you? You gonna go and change out of those wet clothes, or you gonna try for pneumonia and put me to the trouble of paying for your funeral?"

When I come back dry out of my room, she's set up the paper and is staring out the window into the yard. Two rusted hulks of cars sit on blocks out there, one yellow and one green. Jake towed them home and never got around to fixing them. I slip into a chair at the table with her. Finally, Mom looks across at me, her elbow on the table and her chin in her hand.

"Who'd you see in town?" she says.

"Johnny Lang," I say, "and Cousin Charlie."

"Those two!" scoffs my mom. "Did you talk to them?"

"A little."

"What was they doing?"

"They was at Douglas's drinking wine."

"Wonder where they got the money for that? Cheques don't come out 'til Tuesday."

Here is my chance, clear as day, and I still can't tell her. For three days after Jake left for Halifax she ranted and raved and threw things around. She broke a sink full of dishes one afternoon. She heaved the cement block she kept to prop open the kitchen door in the summertime on top of them. I had to pick shards of glass out of the sink and throw them away before we could have supper. I figured if she knew Jake was back in town there might not be enough dishes in the house to do her. We'd have to eat off the table or with sections of the *Banner* laid out underneath us like Jake told me those people across the ocean do with cod and chips. But Jake said to tell her he was coming. It's best if she knows before he shows up at the door. So I take a deep breath and say, loud as lumberjacks, "Jake's back!"

Mom barely stirs. She's looking out the window again. She does that a lot the last week before cheque day. She turns to me and says, "What?"

"Jake's back," I say, not as loud, but trying to get it all out at once. "I saw him outside Douglas's store with Johnny Lang and Charlie Whynot. They was passing around a bottle of wine. Jake bought it. Charlie said Jake's got money now and Johnny said they was going to his cabin on River Road to get drunk. Jake said —"

"You mean my Jake?" Mom says. "Jake McNeil?"

"Jake," I say. "I saw him. With Johnny and Charlie. At Douglas's store."

"You talked to him?"

"Yup."

"Is he back for good?"

"For a visit, he says."

"And what else he say?"

"He said he was comin' out tonight to see us."

"And he's got money, you say?"

"Charlie said so. He said Jake was rich and Jake was buying 'em wine."

"That bastard!" breathes my mother. But I see she's excited, not mad. She jumps up from the table. "Did he say what time he was coming?"

"No. He just said tonight."

She stands in the middle of the floor looking around. Her eye settles on the sink full of dirty dishes. I think about the cement block again. She points at them and tells me to get to work.

"Why?" I say. "Jake don't care 'bout no dishes."

"Don't you question me!" she shouts. "Now you get up there and do the dishes like I told you, or I'll box your ever-lovin' ears."

She runs off to her bedroom to do something — she doesn't say what — and I pull a chair up to the sink and start running the water. There's a lot of dishes and most of them has something dried on them because they've been there for days. It takes me a half hour to do them all and even then some of them aren't completely clean when I put 'em away.

Mom runs around the house straightening up. She even scrubs the kitchen floor with a Wonder Mop. What got into her? Jake had been around as long as I remember and she never washed the kitchen floor on account of him before. Sometimes Jake complained the house was too dirty and Mom told him to clean it himself if he was so particular. Sometimes he did. Now here she is running around like she's on fire, fixing this and that, talking to herself and acting like she hadn't ever heard of Jake McNeil and he's something special come to Sunday dinner. Like he's some great white angel sailing with arms outstretched down the river and come, as Irene Lang says when she comes from Bible study class all worked up about the Lord God Jesus, to deliver us from the error of our ways.

I HAVEN'T BEEN AWAY LONG enough to piss Johnny off, so when he and Charlie ask me to lend them some money I say no problem. Charlie runs inside to get a bottle of Great White, and then Johnny insists I drink it with 'em. We could have stayed in the car, but Johnny has a feud going with old man Douglas. Apparently Douglas tried to tell him he couldn't hang out under the awning of his store, so Johnny wants to go and drink the wine there, just to get up Douglas's nose. I don't want to, but again, with Johnny, you choose your refusals carefully. It starts raining and Nathan comes along. It pisses me off no end that Carla makes him go all the way downtown to pick up a carton of milk and doesn't even bother to make sure he wears the right clothes. I call him over.

"Hiyya Jake."

"Heyya squirt."

Nathan and I shoot the shit for a while, and then Johnny wants more wine and I have to leave. I can see the kid wants more from me — Christ, it's been six months since he's seen me — but I still have to put some time in with Johnny before he'll let me off the hook. So I tell Nathan to go home and I'll see him tonight. Poor kid. I look back at him once, standing there in the middle of the street, shivering in the rain, without a jacket, holding on to the carton of milk for dear life. I feel such a wrench for him in my gut I feel like crying. Johnny's looking at me, like he knows what I'm thinking and despises me for it, and so, to block him, and to think of something else, I whisper under my breath: *the river flows only one way, the river flows only one way, the river flows only one way.*

OUR HOUSE IS THE FIRST one on Harmony Lake Road next to Irene Lang's. It's a little house. Mom rents it from Sam Weare who owns the Esso up the road on Highway #7. Sometimes she don't pay the rent on time and Sam comes down and lectures to her in the kitchen. But he don't hardly ever get mad. Mom sweet-talks him, and he lets us stay. Everyone on our road, except for Irene whose husband works at the mill driving a Pettibone, is on welfare. I know 'cause the welfare worker comes out once a month to see how we're doing and to see if Mom's been applying for jobs. Then she goes to everyone else's house on the road and asks them the same thing. Once when she was new she walked into Irene's house and just sat down and asked her how she was getting along. Irene told Mom the story that same afternoon when I was listening.

"Oh fine," said Irene. "Fine. And you?"

"I'm perfectly fine," said the worker. "It's just the monthly checkup."

"I know," said Irene, who thought the welfare woman just stopped in to be friendly while checking up on everyone else. But when the worker started asking Irene all kinds of questions about money and jobs and working and stuff, Irene threw a fit.

21

"Imagine!" she said to Mom. "She didn't even look at her books or check my name. She just assumed. I sent her out of the house on the toe of my shoe, I can tell you, and not without a call to her manager at the services in town, either."

That night over dinner Mom told the story to Jake. "Serves Irene right," she said. "She thinks she's high and mightier than the rest. Maybe now she knows how it feels not to be, even if it were a mistake."

Mom hates North River. She was born in Oldsport, but she met a guy and "followed him like a dummy." She's been here ever since. Sometimes Jake used to bug her about moving back to Oldsport if she wanted it so bad. She'd just wave him off. "Who's got the money for that? You? Me? Social Services? Uh-uh. Might as well be poor and beholden here as poor and beholden anywhere else, now mightn't I?"

In all the years we've lived in North River I've only been to Oldsport twice. Once was when Jake took me to a car show when I was six, and once was when our school went to the Wool and Carding Museum on Main Street. The car show was the best. Mom was supposed to go, but she got the flu. Jake and I spent the day looking under the hoods of hot rods and eating popcorn. Jake drove me out along the shore in his Pinto to Tyler's Cape afterward. We looked at the fishing boats moored at the government wharf and I found a whole sand dollar on the beach. We had cheeseburgers and french fries for supper at the Dairy Treat and got home later than we were supposed to. Mom was real mad. She screamed at Jake for an hour, though she was still sick. She said Jake was trying to steal me from her and threatened to kick him out. That was no big deal. She was always threatening to kick Jake out.

I WAS FIFTEEN WHEN JOHNNY Lang convinced me to steal my grandfather's rum from his barn one Friday afternoon when he wanted something to drink. My grandfather wasn't religious, at least not like Nana McNeil and Dad, who were always running back and forth to church or talking about the Bible and saying God done this and God done that. My grandfather rarely went to church, unless he went to hear my father preach on Christmas Eve and other holidays. Most Sundays he stayed home. In summer he would go fishing for rainbow trout and salmon in the Memragouche. If he went after church he sometimes took me with him to his favourite hole, which was a deep eddy near the banks not far from the farm where two identical elm trees leaned with crooked boles out over the water. We'd sit our lunch boxes and thermoses in the shadow of the trees to keep 'em cool and bait our lines with the worms he dug from the dung heap behind the barn that morning.

In the winter we would mess around together in the yard, him chopping wood and me stacking it or him tinkering with his International Harvester tractor and me handing him tools. He loved that tractor. He'd had it since 1963 and he told me nothing in the world lasted as long and served you so well as a Harvester International.

"Not even people," he said.

Only I knew my granddad kept a pint bottle of Captain Morgan black rum shoved deep in the barley bin inside the barn. When we were in there together, milking cows or pitching hay, he would stop and wipe a hand across his brow and grin at me.

"Time for a nipper," he'd say, and roll up his sleeve and drive his hand into the sticky barley to the forearm and fish about. Eventually he would bring forth the bottle, wipe it off and take a swig, then bury it again.

"Don't you say nothin' to no one," Granddad McNeil told me. "Your nana is a teetotaller, and wouldn't recommend a drink to a dying man to kill the pain, for fearin' it would be a sin."

"What about Dad?" I asked him.

"Don't tell him either," he spat.

When Johnny was after me I snuck into the barn after dusk and dug around in the barley bin, just like I'd seen my grandfather do all those times. My hand eventually came upon something solid, and I grabbed the bottle and pulled it out. It was nearly full, with barely a drink taken out of it, and I slipped it in my pants and took off out of the barn and down the road as fast as I could go. I don't know what I was thinking. I was the only one my grandfather ever trusted enough to show where he kept his rum.

Sure enough, the next time my father took me out to the farm I went out in the barn to see Granddad McNeil, who was mucking out a stall. He looked at me, nodded and continued cleaning. I got a rake and started helping him. He talked to me all afternoon as usual — joking and making fun and asking me if I was getting any tail and laughing, like he usually did now that

I was older. But when we were done, he did not make right for the barley bin. Instead he took a drink from the dipper from the bucket of well water on the low shelf next to the side door.

"Aren't you gonna have a drink of rum, Granddad?" I asked him. He turned, dipper halfway to his lips, and stared straight at me, as if to tell me he knew, but also that he wasn't going to mention it. "No," he said. "I think I'll just have water for today, Jake. You're welcome to some, if you want it."

My grandfather never took another drink of rum in front of me after that. I checked the barley bin once when I was alone in the barn, but there was no rum in it. I tried a few of the other bins as well, but there was nothing buried there either. Wherever he hid it I never found it, and he never told me. Up until the day he died, nothing changed between us except that. He laughed and joked with me, and got me alone in the barn and asked me about girls and complained about Nana and Dad to me. We were still friends. But I couldn't help feel bad about stealing his rum that time. It wasn't just that I'd taken from him — that was bad enough — but I'd broken something between us that was never fixed. Even after he died it was never fixed. To this day I wish I'd never listened to Johnny Lang and stole that pint of rum out the barley bin.

I'VE NEVER BEEN TO HALIFAX. Jake talked about it some before he left. "It's big," he told me. "And there's lots of lights and buildings. There's traffic running up and down the street at all hours of the night. I don't know how I'm gonna get used to sleeping with all that noise, but I suppose I'll manage."

"Can we come and visit?" I asked him.

"'Course you can, squirt," he told me. "I'll bring you and your mother in as soon as I get settled."

After Jake left I waited to hear from him. We didn't have a phone, but Irene Lang next door did. Jake could have called us on that and Irene would come over and get us. But he didn't call or come and get us for a visit like he said he would. Mom said she knew it all along. "That man ain't good for shit," she said. Mom did get a letter from him twice a month. She wouldn't tell me what it said. Once, when she wasn't looking, I snuck into her purse when she left it on the counter and looked in the envelope. It was a cheque for fifty dollars and a note in Jake's handwriting that said a few words to Mom about boring stuff and then at the bottom, "Tell Nathan hello for me."

I shoved the note back into the purse quick, 'cause Mom came out of the bathroom and nearly caught me. She made me get ready and go with her down to the bank to cash Jake's cheque. She didn't mention she was supposed to say hello. Instead she cursed him the entire two miles we walked into town. "Goddamned good-for-nothing lazy bastard," she said. "What good's fifty dollars gonna do? I gotta get you ready for school, and we gotta eat, and I need things for the house. There he is in the city making good money and sending us peanuts and expecting me to be goddamned grateful. Well, I got news for him. I've half a mind to —"

She never finished so I never knew what she had a half mind to do. I knew better than to ask. But I was happy Jake was thinking of me and hadn't forgotten me, even if he didn't come and get me like he promised. At night I dreamed of the tall glass towers of Halifax, just like Jake described them. I imagined Jake and I walking under them together and sleeping in his apartment at night and getting up and having breakfast together in the morning. I imagined living with Jake, and going to school and meeting new kids and wearing nice clothes and not hand-me-downs from the Salvation Army and the VON.

I think about of all these things again as I do the dishes and Mom runs about the house. I wonder what he has to tell Mom. In my heart there is always the hope Jake has come to get me, to take me with him back to Halifax for good, and I will never see North River and Johnny Lang ever again. But then I hear Mom's voice in my head cursing Jake and saying maybe that's too much to hope for after all, now, isn't it?

JOHNNY'S FATHER BUILT THE CABIN on River Road before he got sent up to Dorchester Penitentiary for aggravated assault in 1967 when Johnny was eleven. Johnny doesn't talk about his father, but Irene Lang told me plenty when I was living beside her at Carla and Nathan's. "He was an awful man," she said to me once. "Scared the living daylights out of me just to be around him. You felt he was looking right through you, like you weren't even there, or didn't matter one whit in his books."

What happened between Johnny and his father is well known in North River. I only heard Johnny mention it once, late one Saturday night in August when everyone had left and I was staying over at his place because Carla and I were fighting and she kicked me out again. Johnny and I were both drunk, and stoned, and finishing off the beer and the last of the Columbian Red in his living room before we went to bed. Out of nowhere Johnny says, "I meant to kill him, you know."

"To kill who?" I thought Johnny meant the guy from Old-sport who almost got the chainsaw enema, but Johnny, sunk deep in his armchair with the last bottle of Alexander Keith's India Pale Ale wedged firmly against his crotch, drunkenly shook his head, as if he knew what I was thinking.

"Him," he said. "*Him*. I meant to do it. I *wanted* to do it."
Johnny passed out then, and never said another word about it,
but I knew then he'd been talking about his father.

The story goes that Johnny's father was released from prison
when Johnny was thirteen, and came right back to North River
from New Brunswick. Johnny's mother was dying of cancer. I
don't remember which kind, but does it matter? My own mother
had cancer of the bowel around the same time, and was shitting
into a colostomy bag and weighed no more than eighty pounds
fully dressed and soaking wet before she died.

By the time Johnny's father came back his mother was end-
stage and bedridden and Johnny had been taking care of things
for almost a year. His aunt Irene came over and helped out when
she could, but Johnny did most of it. And then his father comes
in, starts ordering Johnny around, taking what money they had
and getting drunk and lying around the cabin all day and night
in a stupor. He started taking after Johnny almost right away,
just like he done before he left. One night he picked him up and
hurled him into the fireplace and nearly broke his back. Luckily
it was summer and there wasn't any fire, but Irene figured it
wouldn't have mattered if there had been — John Senior would
have thrown Johnny Junior in anyway.

But the last straw was the night John Senior — Little John,
as everyone called him — took after Johnny's mother. Drunk,
he decided in the middle of the night he wanted some food, and
instead of getting Johnny up he tried to get his sick wife out of
bed. He half-dragged her onto the floor and when she still wouldn't
get up — she was too drugged and delirious to know what was
happening — he went out back, got a pail of cold water from
the well, brought it in and dumped it over her where she lay on
the floor in her nightdress.

29

Johnny watched all this from the doorway to his mother's room. When his father gave up and went back to drinking in the living room, Johnny helped her back into bed and dried her off with a towel. Then he waited until his father passed out in his chair in front of the television, took one of the twelve-gauge shotguns down from the rack in his parents' bedroom and loaded it. He went back into the living room, aimed the gun close range at his father's head and pulled the trigger. Then he called his aunt and told her what he had done.

The story was in all the papers, and for a while Johnny Lang was famous. So was Johnny's mother, who died during her son's trial in juvenile court in Oldsport. Irene Lang made the news when she told a reporter from Halifax the only sin about what happened was that they sent a boy to do a man's job. One of the investigating RCMP officers, who'd had his fair share of run-ins with John Lang Senior over the years, said publicly John Junior deserved a medal for what he did. The trial judge sentenced Johnny to six months in juvenile detention in Spring Hill, and said in his summation that the rule of law forced him to pass a minimum sentence, though if it were up to him Johnny wouldn't spend a half day in jail or a minute more than he had to in his courtroom. Johnny ended up serving the full six months, because he got in a lot of fights at the detention centre, and afterwards was sent home to live with his aunt Irene. He moved back into the cabin when he was seventeen, the year he quit school and got a job at the mill. Irene said she was glad to see him go. She was scared of him, she said. Especially when he was drinking, which he started to do right after reform school.

"Like father, like son," she said. "You'd think going through something like what Johnny had been through would make him a better person, not a worse one."

I know what Johnny would say to that if I told him, and he was willing to talk about it. "This ain't no fuckin' television program, McNeil. What in the fuck do you think seeing your own father's brains scattered all over your living room floor would make you, knowing you pulled the trigger? Mother goddamned fucking Teresa?"

JAKE'S MY FATHER. EVERYONE KNOWS it, but Mom doesn't like for me to say it or call him anything but Jake, so I don't. She met him here, in North River, not long after the guy she followed out from Oldsport left her and went to Cavendish to live with his sister.

Sometimes Mom tells people he was my father. Sometimes she tells them it was some man from the States who had a cottage and lots of money. Only once, when she was drunk, did she say to me who my real father was, though by then I already knew.

"You're just like him," she said, sitting at the kitchen table. She was holding a pint of beer in her lap and nodding her head slowly up and down, as if someone only she could hear was talking to her. I was on the linoleum floor in front of the fridge playing dinky cars. Whenever Mom is drinking she likes to have me around to talk to if there's no one else, though sometimes she forgets I'm there.

"Your father," she said, and waved a hand at the front door, like he was standing outside. "Him! That … that … you know who I mean!"

"Yes Mom," I said.

She shook her head hard from side to side as if I'd said

32

something wrong, or she was trying to clear it of something. She stopped and for a while she didn't say anything else. She hung her head over her beer. I went back to my cars. I liked dinky cars. Mom sometimes got me some for my birthday and one year Jake bought me a whole box of Hotrods for Christmas. I still keep them in the box they came in, all twenty cars stuck sideways in their styrofoam slots. The front of the box has twenty clear plastic windows so you can see each one. My favourite is the souped-up yellow Dodge Charger. It has a breather, lightning decals, mags and a 450 Hemi engine under the hood. I ask Jake how he knows the Charger has a Hemi engine 'cause its hood doesn't open.

"Well it should have one," Jake says, "if it's gonna be any damn good."

Jake used to play dinky cars with me if Mom wasn't around or she was in a good mood, and he would take the Charger and race me with it. He has a beat-up 1972 purple Pinto. Someday he wants to own the souped-up Charger.

"That … that one!" my mother crowed suddenly, making me jump. "Him! Your father. That good-for-nothing, low-down, dirty *bastard* of a man." She struggled to her feet, somehow still managing to hold on to the beer. She just stood there, but now she was looking down at me and I felt scared. Her eyes were red, and hard as marbles. The skin around them was puffed up like it got when she was too drunk. She looked at me like an earwig if it got into the kitchen and she wanted to crush it underfoot.

"You're just like him," she said. "Him and you with your secrets together, and whispering. Don't think I don't hear what you say when you think I'm not listening. I hear. I listen. The two of you making plans against me. Don't think I don't hear it, Mr. Man. Don't think I'm not on to the two of you."

I can't remember what happened next. Maybe she went to

bed and fell asleep and snored the rest of the night. But at least she told me finally, though she would tell me different the next morning. The thing about Mom is, no matter how drunk she gets, she never forgets anything that happens. "About what I said last night," she told me, her eyes still red and puffed, but softer and more tired now. "I was just foolin' ya. Jake isn't really your father, you know."

"I know," I said.

"Good," she said. "I was just talking."

"I know," I said again.

Jake was my father. That much I was sure of, though he never said as much and my mother denied it like Peter denied Jesus before he was nailed to the cross, like Irene Lang told me. Sometimes just by watching Jake I could see me, like I was buried there just underneath his skin, a few inches deep, trying to claw my way out. And sometimes it was just the way Jake looked at me, though in a way his look made me feel worse than Mom's when she got drunk. I'd catch him at it when he thought I wasn't looking — at the table, say, or when we were watching *The Dukes of Hazzard* on Friday night and Mom went out to bingo at the Masonic Lodge with Irene Lang.

I'd look beside me on the couch and Jake would be staring right at me like I done something. Or like he hadn't seen me in a long while. Or like he might not see me ever again.

"What's wrong, Jake?" I'd ask. He'd shake his head and say, "Nothing," and turn back to the TV. But I could tell it was something. I knew. It wasn't just me Jake was looking at like that, like I caught him by surprise by even being there and being alive. It was himself he was looking at, buried in me just like I was buried in him.

Even Mom has to admit she sees that much about us.

TWICE JOHNNY SENDS ME AND Charlie back to the liquor store for more White Shark and by three o'clock they are so pie-eyed they can barely see three feet in front of them. And yet, every time I make noises about going, Johnny tells me to sit the fuck still. "What's your hurry, McNeil? You got a dinner party to go to?"

Sometimes Johnny gets in these moods and there isn't any point arguing with him. You have to wait him out. If I play along long enough, he'll see I've had enough and let me go. So I sit and wait. He doesn't seem to notice I'm not drinking much.

Or maybe he noticed and doesn't mind — all the more for him if I don't. Johnny is flat broke. He quit working at the mill years ago. He is on welfare, and sells enough hash and weed and the occasional sheet of acid to keep him drunk and high most of the time. But the dope business hasn't been so good lately. The RCMP seized a big shipment of Columbian coming in off the coast of Oldsport and Johnny's supply has dried up.

He has some, though, 'cause he keeps pulling out a baggie and rolling joints. I take it each time it comes to me, take a few half-hearted puffs and pass it on. When Johnny pulls out three tabs of purple microdot and tells Charlie and I to each take one, I refuse.

35

"Sorry, man," I say. "I gotta go see the old man and Carla tonight. I can't be too fucked up, ya know?"

Johnny doesn't say nothing. Charlie pops one tab and Johnny pops the last two. Then he leans back in his chair and squints at me. I feel uncomfortable, but there is nothing I can do. I'll never get out of here if I take that stuff and, besides, I never really liked it. I feel too out-of-control on acid. I remember one time freaking out on it and running into the woods behind Johnny's house in the middle of the night. I stayed in there five hours and hallucinated all kinds of crazy shit. I saw an old hag dressed in rags with long stringy grey hair scramble up a tree and look down and cackle at me. I saw a deer with eyes as big as saucers. I found a place to curl up and close my eyes and wait for the acid to wear off. I came out at dawn to find Johnny and Charlie and a bunch of others sitting up in Johnny's house still tripping. They took one look at me, with pine needles stuck to my clothes and in my hair, and started laughing their asses off.

Johnny don't look none too happy, but he doesn't force me to do the acid. Charlie's chin drops to his chest as he sits there mumbling to himself. He isn't asleep, just so drunk he can't hold his head up. Charlie gets this way at a certain point in the day, though at any moment he can snap out of it and start talking and drinking like he was before. Johnny seems to get more comfortable in his chair and is staring off at the wall at a point just above my head. We sit that way for what seems like close to a half hour with nobody saying nothing. The clock above the sink says it's five o'clock. I tell Johnny I have to go.

His eyes slide down from whatever he is staring at to crawl across my face. "Sure, man," he says. "Just hold on second."

I can tell the acid is working in Johnny when he has trouble getting out of his chair. It isn't the kind of trouble you have when you're drunk. It's like he thinks the chair is gonna float away on him if he isn't careful. He gets out of it gingerly, and says, "I'll be right back."

He disappears into the bedroom.

I think about splitting right then. I might make it to the car before Johnny wises up, and he doesn't have any wheels to follow me. I'd have to be careful whenever I came back into North River but at least I'd be free of him.

In the end, I don't have the guts to move outta my chair.

MY MIDDLE NAME IS ALEXANDER. Mom says Jake gave it to me. He wanted it to be my first name, "after some dumb Greek he read about somewhere," but Mom wouldn't let him. "Alexander's too damn long," she said, "and Alex is a girl's name." Mom told me this once when she was in a good mood, when she forgot, I guess, Jake wasn't supposed to be my father.

"He was just around at the time," she said when she caught herself. "I let him help with the naming."

When Mom told me this last year I looked up the dumb Greek in an encyclopedia at school. The only Greek guy in there was Alexander the Great and it turns out he wasn't really Greek at all but from a place called Macedonia that the Greeks didn't like because they thought everyone who lived there was stupid, kind of like the way Nova Scotians feel about people from Newfoundland. I wondered at the time if the Greeks made up Macedonian jokes, like how many Macedonians did it take to screw in a light bulb, until I remembered light bulbs weren't invented then. We learned all about Thomas Edison that year in school. His father was from Nova Scotia, but I was sure I remembered he was from New York. I didn't know how close New York was to Macedonia but I had no one to ask. Mom would get mad if I asked her, and Jake was off in the woods that winter cutting trees with a crew. It was still neat knowing Jake gave me that name.

It said in the book that Alexander the Great beat up almost all of the world and took it all over — though he never made it as far as Canada because he didn't know where it was on the map. It said he was a great warrior, the greatest ever, and after he beat all those people up and killed the soldiers and raped the wives and took over the land he was kind and just and a good king.

Whenever I think of my middle name I feel good about it some-how. I whisper it to myself sometimes when no one's around: *Alexander.* It's like Jake has buried something special right inside me somehow by naming me that, like there's this great warrior caught between my first name and my last, waiting to come out.

Whenever things go bad I try to think of him and what a great fighter like him would do in my place.

WHEN I WAS FIVE I fell in my grandfather's barn. I liked to go into the loft because I liked the smell of the hay. He stored it in stacked bales ten high and when he needed some he and I would climb up and he'd let me help throw the bales down to the floor of the barn and watch them break open then pull them into rows to pitch to the cows. But sometimes I would go up alone and climb the bales and sit at the top and breathe in the smell of the fresh-cut hay and watch the hay dust drift into the shafts of light cutting in from the barn windows. My grandnan didn't like me in there. She was afraid I would fall, but Grandad didn't mind as long as I was careful. But one time climbing the tallest stack of hay in the loft I lost my footing, grabbed hold of a bale to keep from falling, and the whole stack came down. I landed on my back and the bales tumbled down in a pile on top of me.

Later everyone said it was lucky I didn't break a bone, or my back. Granddad said there must have been ten bales or more on top of me when he found me. But I wasn't hurt. I lay there smelling the warm hay, feeling its weight on top of me, wondering about the darkness because the bales had sealed me off from the world and the light. I wasn't scared. It was the first time I remember thinking it was strange how the world could go

40

from one way to another in a minute, from one simple misstep. From light and air to darkness and heaviness and the smell of hay so close around me it pressed in like a blanket. I've thought of that many times since. I didn't fight my way out from under the hay. I lay there for what seemed like hours, until my granddad came up to check on me and found me under the hay and lifted it all off and set me free.

"You gave us half a scare, boy," he said later. "Thought you were dead for a minute."

I never told my granddad I could have made my own way out from underneath the hay any time I wanted. That I didn't because I liked the darkness, and the smell, and I knew things under the hay I couldn't have known at any other time. I was only five.

WHEN I WAS FIVE I almost died.

Mom said it was something called a "summer complaint." I got all filled up and couldn't breathe and they took me to the Oldsport hospital. A whole bunch of doctors and nurses put needles in my arms and took my temperature.

I was really scared. Jake and Mom weren't allowed to see me, because the doctors thought they might get it too. The doctors and nurses who came into my room had to wear masks. The nurses were really nice, but I still wanted to go home. I couldn't sleep at night. There was too much light, and the nurses kept coming in and waking me up. Once during the day I fell asleep and when I woke up Jake was sitting beside my bed with a white mask over his mouth and nose. It looked like he was crying.

"What's wrong, Jake?" I asked.

"Nothing, squirt," he said. "How you feeling?"

"I want to go home, Jake," I said.

"Soon, squirt," he said. "Soon."

I was in the hospital for almost a whole week and when I went home I didn't have to go to school in September when it started. I was home for almost two months. The principal wanted to keep me back because I missed too much but Mom fought with him and they let me in. My first day back everyone talked about how I was almost dead.

"Hey shithead!" one of the older kids said to me on the playground at recess. "Heard you almost kicked the bucket!"

I didn't know what "kicked the bucket" meant. Jake had to explain it to me. For a while everyone was really nice. Even Mom. But then she got tired of having me under her feet and made me get dressed in my snowsuit one afternoon and go outside and play with the other kids. Mom always said I should go out and play with the other kids though there was no one else to play with on our road. Jake got mad and said I was still too sick to be outside in the snow. Mom told him I was her son and not his and she could do whatever she wanted. Jake and her started screaming and Jake got so mad he left and didn't come home for three days. That was no big deal. Jake was always taking off for two or three days after he and Mom got in one of their fights. Each time it happened I worried he wouldn't come back. When Jake wasn't around things were too quiet in our house. But Jake always did come back. He'd show up like normal one morning. I'd get outta bed and go to the kitchen and there Jake would be, sitting with Mom at the kitchen table, smoking and drinking coffee.

"Heyya squirt," he'd say as if he hadn't been anywhere at all. He and Mom would be talking quietly about anything except their fight and the fact we hadn't seen Jake for days. For a while things would be okay between them. I liked these times. I could sit between my mother and Jake at the table and eat my Frosted Flakes and not worry one of them was going to get mad and start yelling. Sometimes Jake reached out and mussed my hair. Mom didn't say anything, though normally she didn't like Jake

43

to touch me. I loved it when Jake touched me. It made me feel all good inside, like I was sitting next to a wood stove and outside it was storming real bad, but inside I was warm and safe. That's how having Jake touch me made me feel.

THE LATE AFTERNOON SUNLIGHT BREAKS through the clouds and filters duskily down through the trees and in through the patio doors at the front of the cabin. The fire crackles and sparks in the hearth. Outside I can hear the river gushing moodily over the falls. Suddenly I see Nathan's face in my mind's eye, as clear as day. He is smiling at me the way he does sometimes when we're alone, his head turned a little to one side like his mother does when she wants something. Only Nathan doesn't want anything. Except for the one thing I want too, the thing we don't mention or speak about or even dream could happen.

If I can get away from Johnny and the hell out of North River for good, maybe I can give it to him.

JAKE'S MY ONLY FRIEND. I used to have one in Grade Two named Tommy, but he moved to Trenton when his mom and dad got a divorce. Jake and Mom never got a divorce.

I asked Jake about this once. He said people only get a divorce if they're married, and Jake and Mom didn't get married. In school once we did a report on our parents. Everyone got up in front of the class and told about their mother and father. When they were born. When they met. When they were married and stuff like that. I didn't know what to do. I could have written about Jake but I was worried Mom would find out and take after me. I worried and worried about that report. I didn't know what to write. In the end I just wrote about Mom and not about Jake. When I finished, my teacher, Mrs. Burns, asked me to go ahead and do my father. I was really embarrassed. I didn't know what to say. All the other kids laughed and Mrs. Burns told them to be quiet. She told me I could sit down. After that kids started saying I didn't have any father. They said a seagull jerked off on a rock and the sun hatched me. I didn't know what jerked off was so I asked Jake.

"Where did you hear that?" he said.

I told him about the report, and what happened. I was

worried I would hurt Jake's feelings when he found out I didn't write about him. But he just smiled. "I wouldn't worry about those assholes in your class," Jake said. "You know who your father is, don't you?"

"Yes Jake," I said.

"That's all that matters then," Jake said.

That was the closest Jake and I ever came to talking about it.

UP NORTH ON THE LOGGING crew I was a marker. I would walk around the woods all day with a green knapsack on my back stuffed with rolls of neon orange surveyor's tape and tie lengths of it around the trunks of trees, marking them for the rest of the crew to cut down. Some days I would mark two hundred trees or more — birch and oak and tamarack and spruce and pine and poplar and maple and anything else big enough to feel the bite of the saw. In the distance I could hear the shouts of the crew and the snarl of their power saws, the idling of the boom trucks as they were loaded to haul the logs back to North River. Other times I went so deep into the woods I couldn't hear anything. The snow was deep, and I wore rubber boots and hip waders to keep myself dry. At lunch I stopped and ate sandwiches from my knapsack and washed them down with hot coffee laced with cream and sugar from a thermos. It got so that I felt a part of the woods. Deer would pick their way delicately through the deep snow and barely stop to look at me. Once, in the early part of the year, a black bear lumbered by, in its last full days before it crawled into a cave to sleep until spring. Squirrels scampered along lengths of branches above me and scolded as I passed. Ravens cawed from the tops of Scotch pines. Porcupines and rabbits sat back on their haunches and stared curiously at me from the ground.

I thought a lot.

It was funny how much I thought. My mother used to say I was a boy who liked my own company, and that was as true then as it ever was. I imagined all kinds of things — normal things, like being famous, or rich, or getting a blow job from a blonde with huge tits I once saw in Oldsport, the kind of girl who did not exist in North River and, it seemed, never would. Not normal things, like living in a world without trees where everything was flat and tan and green, or travelling in a one-man, glass-sided spaceship past Pluto, the small blue ice planet I learned about in science class in Grade Nine and somehow never forgot. I thought about my mother, and Jerry Rowter, a boy from my class who died in a car accident in Grade Eleven. I tried to imagine what it would be like to be a bear, and get fat and sleep for seven months out of the year in a cave, or be a squirrel, and collect nuts and live in the trunk of a tree. And of course I thought about Nathan.

I wrote him letters in my head.

Dear Nathan. I am your father.

Dear Nathan. I wish the two of us could travel in a glass ship together to the edges of space.

Stupid stuff. Stuff I would never tell anyone about, except maybe the blonde.

At the end of the day I would come back to the camp, as tired from my thoughts as from fighting through all that snow and reaching around the trunks of trees to tie tape all day. I would have dinner with the crew, who would tease me and call me Grizzly Adams 'cause I was growing a beard, and ask me what I did out there by myself in the woods all day and didn't

49

I think I might go blind from it? I laughed with them, 'cause they were good men, and didn't mean no harm. After supper we drank rum and played whist in front of the stove, and crawled in our bunks around the same time and shot the shit in the darkness for an hour or so before falling off to sleep. That was the only time I ever remember belonging and feeling right about things my whole life, probably because I had all that time in the day to be by myself and think about things.

MY FATHER WAS BORN IN 1957.

His birthday is November 14th.

He drives a purple Pinto. He says the Pinto is a piece of shit. He would rather have a Dodge Charger.

My father has light brown hair and brown eyes. His hair is always hanging in his eyes.

He wears a black leather jacket.

He used to work at the mill in North River.

He used to work in the woods on a logging crew.

Now he works at the Dockyards in Halifax.

I'm not supposed to tell anyone he is my father.

I would like to be like him when I grow up.

AFTER I GRADUATED HIGH SCHOOL I went to university in Halifax for one year. It was my father's idea. It cost a lot of money to go. My grades were good but not good enough to get a scholarship. I got a student loan. My old man said he wanted me to get a decent job and not end up at the mill like every other guy my age in North River.

"What's wrong with the mill?" I asked him.

"Nothing," he said, "if you want to blister your hands and strain your back and work for minimum wage for the rest of your life."

So I went. I didn't know what to take. I always read a lot — my favourite writer was Stephen King — so my old man suggested I study English. I sent off an application to the University of King's College in Halifax, where my father knew someone. It was an Anglican school, and though my old man was Baptist, he thought it would be a good idea if I went to a school where there was an outside chance I would go to church once in a while, no matter whose church it was.

I hated college from the first minute I got there. All the other students were from rich families, and drove nice cars, and a lot of them went to private schools and had their own credit cards.

I didn't even have my own bank account. I took the Foundation Year Program where they assigned all these authors I'd never heard of — Sophocles and St. Augustine and Thomas Hobbes. They bored me to tears. I wore a leather jacket and my hair was long. Everyone else had nice coats and polo shirts and cut their hair short. Most of the time I wandered around in a daze, wondering how the hell I had gone from reading *The Shining* to *The Confessions* in such a short time.

Some of the guys in my dorm saw I was struggling. They tried to help me through it. They came into my room and asked me how it was going and offered to read over my papers and told me to take it slow and not get caught up in not having a Jaguar.

It didn't work. By December I was flunking, and when I went home for Christmas I told my father I wasn't going back.

"Why?" my father asked me.

"Because," I told him. "It's not for me. The work's too hard, and the people are not my kind of people."

"What is your kind of people, Jake?" my dad said. "Johnny Lang? Charlie Whynot?"

"At least," I said, "they don't put on airs."

"What you call airs," my father said, "I call being educated. You're never going to get anywhere with this attitude."

We fought about it, and for Christmas that year my father gave me a yellow hard hat and a pair of work gloves. He meant it as an insult, but I didn't give him the satisfaction.

"Thanks," I said. "These will come in handy."

That was the year I met Carla, and she got pregnant with Nathan. I moved in with her and out of my father's house. He still talked about college sometimes, saying I messed up a great opportunity and that my mother would be disappointed if she was alive. I didn't bother to argue with him about it. I did go to work at the mill that March, and my father was right. It was hard labour, and sometimes I came home so bone-tired I could barely find the strength to eat.

My job was a poler. I would stand on a raft in the middle of the log pond and peavey-pole logs onto the chain, where they would get carried up to the first saw before they went to the re-saw further inside the mill. I had a lot to think about, standing there and herding logs onto the chain all day. I thought about some of the books we read in college, and the only one I liked, which was this play by an Italian guy named Pirandello called *Six Characters in Search of an Author*. It was about these characters in a play who were lost on stage, and one of their kids gets killed. The sad part of the story was once the play was over you realized all these characters were doomed to repeat this same story over and over again, with the same tragedy, because they had yet to be written.

Sometimes that's the way I felt in North River. Like we were all living the same lives over and over again, with no way out, with no one to write us. I had my chance, I suppose, but I blew it when I quit university.

That's why I went to Halifax the second time.

To be written.

I'M SCARED OF MY SCHOOL.

Sometimes the older boys catch me on school grounds when the teacher isn't looking and give me noogies and Indian rope burns. They call me names. They say my mother is a whore and we don't own a pot to piss in. They all have nice houses on Cobb's Ridge. Cobb's Ridge is where all the rich kids live.

Once Jake went to the principal of our school when I told him what was happening at recess and asked him what he was going to do about it. The principal's name was Mr. Sheppard.

"Do about what?" Mr. Sheppard said.

I had a black eye that day. I told Jake one of the boys in school gave it to me.

"This," Jake said, pushing me towards Mr. Sheppard. "This has got to stop. The kids beat up on him."

Mr. Sheppard looked at me then back at Jake. "I'm afraid, Jake," he said, "that Nathan came to school with that particular bruise on Monday morning. I assure you he did not get it on school grounds."

Jake looked at me, and then at Mr. Sheppard. He looked like he didn't know what to say.

"It's not the first time he's come to school with marks on him," Mr. Sheppard said.

Jake sent me out of the office. He and Mr. Sheppard stayed in there a long time talking. After a while Jake came out again. He barely spoke on the way home. But before we turned onto Harmony Lake Road, Jake asked me why I told him the kids in school gave me the black eye.

"They did give it to me," I said.

Jake didn't say anything. That night he and Mom fought. There was a lot of screaming and shouting. Jake threatened to take me away. He said he wouldn't go to work on the tree-cutting crew anymore because Mom couldn't be trusted when he was gone. But the next morning when I woke up Jake had left again to go up north. He wouldn't be back for a whole week.

"Where's Jake?" I asked my mom.

"Never mind," she said. "Eat your breakfast."

Except there wasn't any breakfast. I had to make it myself.

I REGRET STAYING THE MINUTE Johnny comes back out the bedroom with a twelve-gauge shotgun in his hands. Is it the same gun he killed his father with? I decide it isn't. The police would have confiscated that one, wouldn't they? Johnny is smiling and looking straight at me as he sits down in the chair with the gun laid across his lap. Its barrel is pointing directly at Charlie, who is still on the nod and mumbling away to himself, oblivious.

"It's loaded," he says. "In case you think I'm foolin' ya and didn't put a shell in it. Do you think I'm foolin' ya?"

His blue eyes look a little wild, the pupils dilated. The two hits of purple microdot are working in him good. I slowly shake my head to Johnny's question.

"Good," he says. "Now, if you say one more word about havin' to leave before I tell you it's okay to leave, or you try and take off when you think I'm not looking, I'm gonna blow a hole in you the size of an oil barrel cover. You got it?"

I nod, and again say nothing. My mouth is too dry *to* say anything. I'm scared but I'm not surprised. It is as if I'd always known our relationship would come to this.

Johnny lights up a smoke and offers me one. I quit over a

year ago, but something tells me it wouldn't be wise to refuse. Also, under the circumstances, I need one. I take the smoke and Johnny, leaning over the gun in his lap, holds the Bic up for me so I can light it. It tastes awfully good, like when I was a kid and first learned how to smoke without getting sick. For something to say, I tell him this.

"Yeah," he says. It's like the gun's not even there, we're acting so calm and normal. "Every once in a while you have one like that. It tastes so goddamned good it reminds you of the first cigarette you ever smoked."

I nod, except the first cigarette I ever smoked didn't taste so good. I was eleven and it was with my friend Eugene, who moved away a few years after. I inhaled the whole thing and was so dizzy and sick I had to lie down by the side of the road 'til it went away. I swore right then I would never smoke again, though, of course, it didn't stick. Promises made like that never do.

I ask Johnny about the first cigarette he ever smoked. It makes sense to me to keep him talking, to keep things even between us and not act too scared. Maybe then he will put the gun up and let me go. Johnny scowls. "It was with the ol' man. I was eight or so, and we was huntin' and he gave me one. I didn't want it, but he made me. He called me a goddamned pussy and bugged me 'til I lit up. Right from the first, though, I liked it, and I used to steal 'em from his pack when he wasn't lookin'. I used to think it served the bastard right for makin' me have one when I didn't want to."

Charlie wakes up. He shouts something we can't make out, and Johnny and I both jump. It's lucky Johnny's finger isn't on the trigger, 'cause the bore is pointing at Charlie. Charlie lifts his head, opens his eyes, and looks at us blearily. He reaches out for the pack of smokes on the coffee table, though he can't be seeing well, 'cause he keeps missing them.

"Light one for 'im, will ya?" Johnny says to me.

I do, and hand it to Charlie. He takes it in the hand without the glove and shivers like he's cold, though Johnny has a fire going in the fireplace, and it's hot as Hades in there.

Johnny picks up the gun, puts it to his shoulder, and aims at Charlie's head. "What do you think, McNeil? Put ol' Charlie here out of his misery?"

Charlie doesn't even notice. He keeps one arm wrapped around his waist, leaning forward and staring at the table and sucking away on his cigarette. I figure it's best not to say anything while Johnny sights up Charlie's head in the bead.

"Blam!" says Johnny, and lowers the gun. He reaches over and tousles Charlie's hair. "He's a good boy, ol' Charlie."

Charlie keeps staring at the one spot on the table, shivering and acting as if he hasn't heard.

Maybe he hasn't. I figure he's seeing and hearing shit from the acid. Just then Johnny decides he has to go take a piss. "But what am I gonna do with you?" he says. He turns to Charlie, looks as if he is considering giving the gun to him, and then changes his mind. Charlie's so out of it he won't be able to see to keep a bead on me. He turns back to me. "Remember that little window in the bathroom?" he says. "The one looks out onto the driveway?"

"Yeah," I say.

"Well, you try to leave, and think of me, leaning over the toilet taking a piss with the barrel of this gun hanging out that window and my finger on the trigger. You won't make it to your car."

"Jesus, Johnny," I say, feeling more scared suddenly than I had been. "Why are you doing this?"

"Because," Johnny answers. "You ain't the same, McNeil. The city's changed you, and I figure it's my job to change you back, or have you die trying." Johnny laughs at his own joke, and hoists the shotgun up over his shoulder, soldier-style. "Remember that little window," he says, "and think of me if you try to leave."

ONCE JAKE AND I WATCHED the total eclipse of the sun.

An eclipse is when the moon passes between the Earth and the sun and blocks it.

"The sun is bigger than we can imagine," Jake said.

"How big is the moon then?" I asked him.

"Smaller than the Earth," Jake said, "but still pretty big."

"So how can the moon block the sun if it's smaller than it?"

Jake said that was a good question. He ruffled my hair and said I was smart. Mom didn't watch the eclipse. She said she didn't have time for stars-and-moon foolishness. She stayed inside and did laundry and drank beer. It was in January, and kind of cold.

We spent all afternoon getting ready for it. Jake said we couldn't look directly at it because we would go blind, but he made this thing out of Coke bottle glass and a piece of paper to watch it with.

We watched on the paper as the shadow of the moon crawled across the face of the sun.

At one point it got so dark it was like it was night out.

It was so quiet.

It was like the world stopped breathing.

Jake held my hand.

It seemed like the two of us stood there forever in the darkness while the moon ate up the sun.

JOHNNY IS IN THE BATHROOM so long I nod off in the chair. I dream my father and I are fishing on the Memragouche River up by the Sandbanks Cemetery. He's wearing his hip waders and standing midway out in the water, casting his line. I am on the shore with my little rod and reel and worm bait, and my father keeps shouting back to me to see how I'm doing.

I am six or seven in the dream, and it might be more of a memory, because my dad and I used to do this a lot before my mother died.

Then suddenly, in my dream, I am in the hip waders, casting the line and looking back. I see Nathan behind me on the shore with the rod and reel. Nathan is smiling. Behind him is Johnny Lang with a shotgun to his head.

I wake up sweating, and remember where I am. Johnny, the son-of-a-bitch, is still not out of the bathroom.

ALL AFTERNOON MOM PACES THE house waiting for Jake to show up. She can't sit still in front of *Another World*, although she never misses a show if she can help it. I try to stay out of her way. I read *Archie Digest* in my room but she keeps coming in and asking me things.

"What's he look like?" she says to me the first time this happens.

"What's who look like?"

"Jake, you dummy!"

I shrug. "He looks like Jake."

"What was he wearing, then?"

"His leather."

"The same leather?"

"It could have been the same. Or it might have been different. I don't know."

"Some help you are," Mom says, and stomps out of my room. Another time she comes and asks me exactly what time he said he was coming.

"He didn't say," I tell her. "He just said tonight."

"Late tonight or early tonight?"

"I don't know. He didn't say."

A few times I think she's gonna get mad but she never does.

She goes back out to the kitchen and walks the floor some more. At four o'clock, after *Another World* is over, Irene Lang comes for a visit. "That Iris," says Irene as soon as she gets through the front door. "What a piece of work that is, isn't it?"

"I didn't watch the stories today," Mom says, and tells Irene all about Jake being back in town and me seeing him with Johnny and Charlie at Douglas's. They forget all about *Another World*. I go out and sit on the floor in a corner and listen to them. Irene is curious why Jake has come back.

"Has he left anything here?" she says. "Clothes, or the like, that needs to be picked up?"

"He ain't left a thing, as far as I know," Mom says.

"Does he owe anything? Anything that couldn't be paid by cheque?"

"Not that I know."

"Maybe he's come back to see his father?"

"Jake? He'll see him all right, but he wouldn't make a trip special to see that old coot. The two of them get along about as well as fire and water."

Irene looks sideways at me, sitting in the corner looking up at them, and bites her tongue. It's clear as day Mom thinks Jake's come back to see her and clear as two days Irene doesn't. When the kettle is hot Mom pours them both a cup of tea and Irene goes on about her nephew.

"Well, if he does have any money, like Nathan says, it's a sure bet he'll be broke by the time he gets in tonight. Johnny'll have him sucked dry as a Baptist supper come evening."

"Jake can handle himself next to the likes of Johnny Lang," Mom says. "He'll come with money, don't you worry."

"Well, I certainly hope so. But that Johnny has all the ways of the devil and then some for getting what he wants. I've not seen the beat of him for using and abusing other people. Just like his father, he is. God knows what ever possessed me to go and marry Tom and tie us up with a family like that for all time."

Mom isn't listening. She's staring out the window into the driveway as if she expects Jake's purple Pinto to turn into it at any time. Irene settles her eye on me.

"You glad to see Jake again, Nathan?"

"Yup," I tell her. "Jake says he's gonna take me to Halifax to visit him sometime."

"Don't count on that," Mom says without turning from the window. "Jake's none too good on keeping promises."

Then Irene does something strange. She winks at me. It's strange seeing an old woman like Irene wink, especially 'cause she goes to Bible class and all. I don't know what she means. She looks away before I can ask. "Well, I should be getting back. I've got a load of clothes in the wash, and Tom'll be wanting his supper when he gets home."

"What you having?" Mom asks, but like she doesn't care about the answer.

"Corned beef and cabbage," says Irene, sighing and getting to her feet. "Picked up the beef on special from the IGA last week. Tom's favourite."

"Ay-yuh," Mom says, and Irene turns to go. But before she does she looks at me again and nods, like she knows something Mom and I don't. "Come on up and see me sometime, Alexander," she says. "I've got a tin of biscuits in the cupboard with your name on it."

"I will," I tell her.

Irene leaves, though Mom hardly seems to notice. She sits and stares out the window from the kitchen table and I slink back to my room to read comics. But my heart is beating fast and I'm excited. Mom didn't notice that Irene called me by my secret name, by Jake's name. That is the first time anyone besides Jake called me that. It's as if Irene knows — knows that some great storm is coming to tear me out of Macedonia and into the great wide world.

CHARLIE IS STILL ASLEEP AND mumbling away to himself and twitching like a crazy man on the sofa. Suddenly he wakes up again and looks at me. He looks halfways sober this time. "Where's Johnny?" he says.

"Bathroom."

Charlie nods. Asks me for a smoke. I point to them on the table. Charlie leans over slow as an old man and takes one and tries to light it. His hands are shaking so bad he can't touch the flame to the cigarette, and so I reach over, pry the lighter from his hand and do it for him. He leans back, takes a long drag, and sighs as he exhales the smoke.

His eyes are closed.

I feel sorry for Charlie. He's Carla's cousin but she don't ever have him over. His own mother doesn't let him past her front door 'cause he's stolen from her purse too many times for money for booze and dope. No one knows where his father is. He left 'em when Charlie was just a kid. Most times he stays at Johnny's house but sometimes he'll sleep at another friend's if they don't mind him on the sofa for a few days.

He's twenty-nine, but he looks forty.

And he's dumb.

In school he was in my class for a year until I passed and he got held back again for the third time. Sometimes I'd try and help him with his homework. He could never get it, and quit eventually. He didn't have a car. He was picked up by the RCMP a couple of times a year for being drunk and disorderly, and they drove him to Oldsport and threw him in the drunk tank for the night. Everyone says Charlie Whynot is a bum, and he'll be dead by the time he's forty.

They're probably right, but still. I remember when we were kids together, and he could be kind of funny. He had more guts than any of us, even Johnny. If you dared Charlie to do something, he would do it. No questions asked.

"Johnny's acting funny today," I say, hoping Charlie will help me.

He doesn't look up at me. He's staring at his own lap, still smoking the cigarette. "Any more White Shark?" he says finally.

"It's all gone," I say. "Did you hear me? I said Johnny's acting funny. He's got a gun out and he won't let me leave."

Charlie looks up at me then, but I'm still not sure he understands. "What's the city like, Jake? You like it there?"

"It's all right, Charlie, but …"

"I should go," he says. "Get outta North River. Nothing tying me here, 'cept Johnny. They got girls there? Nice ones?"

"Lots of 'em. But Charlie. I need you to help me with Johnny."

Charlie still acts like he doesn't hear. Maybe he doesn't. "I had a girl once. You remember her? Jane Marie Wambolt. Cute. Kinda fat, but cute. She could fuck too, Jake. Near wore me out she did. I never see her anymore. She still around here?"

I shake my head. "I don't know, Charlie."

He isn't going to be any help. He's still too high to know what's going on, and even if he wasn't he'd likely just get himself in shit if he said anything. Johnny doesn't punch Charlie, or threaten him. He doesn't have to. Charlie's no threat.

I watch as Charlie finishes his smoke, then watch as his head inches forward and he falls asleep again. I feel such a blackness of mood wash over me. Maybe today is the day Johnny gets to kill somebody else and maybe that somebody will be me. Maybe he and Charlie will cut me up into little pieces with the Husqvarna and it will be weeks before anyone traces me out here and finds the pieces.

But find them they will. I have no doubt about that. Johnny has one more murder in him, and then he's gonna get caught and sent away for good, and maybe then North River will be safe. It's too bad I have to be the unlucky bastard Johnny Lang nails to a fucking cross in order for everyone else to be saved.

JAKE'S FATHER IS AN INDIAN.

"Only part Indian," Jake tells me, but that doesn't matter.

It means I'm part Indian, too.

I have dreams sometimes where we are all living in teepees and hunting and fishing and there are no cars or airplanes.

Jake used to take me fishing.

It was in South River, where these two trees with funny shapes leaned out over the water and we'd put our lunches and water bottles in the shadow of the trees out of the heat. Jake'd tell me stories and sometimes we'd come home with trout for my mother.

My mother loves trout.

I'd hold them on a stick while Jake slit open their bellies with a jackknife and removed the guts. I'd stare into their dead fish eyes when he did it. Thinking I was glad I wasn't a trout. Thinking I was glad I was part Indian, and how someday I'd like to ride in a birchbark canoe.

WHEN JOHNNY COMES OUT OF the bathroom I am so restless I can barely sit still in my chair. I think he's stayed in there so long because he wants me to get antsy. He wants me to try and leave so he can shoot me. The acid is working in him hard now. I can see by his eyes things are starting to change. They aren't good changes either.

"Get up," Johnny says to me. He still holds the gun down at his waist, but he waves it threateningly towards me.

"Why, Johnny?" I say. "I've been sitting here like you asked me."

"Get the fuck up, McNeil. We're going for a walk."

By now Charlie is passed out again. I can't understand how he can sleep with a whole hit of acid in his blood, but he's snoring away, curled up like a baby on Johnny's sofa, his back to us. Johnny looks at him once and then back at me. I am on my feet like Johnny asked, but standing there, looking at him. "Johnny, man," I say. "What you gonna do?"

"That depends on you," says Johnny.

I can see I am fucked. Somehow, Johnny has convinced himself I am the enemy, that I have done something to him, even if he can't say what that something is. I give up, turn, and go outside.

It stopped raining hours ago, but I left my coat inside and it's cold. I ask Johnny if I can go back and get it.

"You won't be needing it," he says. "Get going."

He herds me across the driveway and across to the walking bridge over the river below his house. The river here is narrow, but too fast for a boat, and his father built the bridge out of mooring rope and old dory planks years ago so he wouldn't have to walk up to Eight-Mile Bridge to get across to hunt. I hated walking across that bridge with Johnny when I was young. It swayed when you went, and there were big gaps between the boards and I was afraid it was going to let go. Now, for the first time, I was hoping it would, as Johnny told me to walk across it with the gun at my back. I kept looking down so I wouldn't miss the boards, and for a minute I thought of this other book we read in college, called *Inferno*, by this other Italian guy named Dante. He wrote all about these people dying and being herded across this river called Styx, where on the other side this monster with a long tail would wrap it around them and then toss them into whatever circle of hell held their punishment.

Dante was a sick fucker.

People got burnt alive, or eaten by birds called harpies, or had to eat each other and then crap each other out, or were buried up to their necks in shit forever.

I try not to think about it.

On the other side of the bridge there is a narrow worn path. In the fall when Johnny and I go deer hunting this is the way we come. Johnny built a blind in a clearing about a quarter mile back, and we used to sit and smoke and wait for the deer to wander out. Even as kids we used to go there with our BB guns and shoot squirrels. I ask Johnny if this is where we are going. Johnny says nothing, except to tell me to keep moving. I'm trying to think of ways I can get out of this. I'm not so scared anymore. For some reason, the dream I had about Nathan and my father when Johnny was in the bathroom made me feel stronger, just as it now makes me want to get out of this somehow. Johnny is gonna try and kill me. There is no use pretending otherwise. Never mind it doesn't make a lick of sense. Later he'll blame it on the acid, and that I kept trying to get away from him.

"Hey man," I say. "You remember the time we sent Charlie back here in the middle of the night to check your rabbit snares, and we came in after him and made noises like we were ghosts?"

Johnny stays quiet.

"Remember how he shit his pants, and went running off the path and scraped his face and hands all up? You remember that?"

The path hasn't been used much this year — it's overgrown in places. I keep having to push wet branches out of my way, and then hold them back for Johnny, because he's right behind me with the gun. I'm getting soaked, because every time I move a branch, water from the tree drips down on my shoulders and soaks my hair and shirt.

"Hey Johnny," I say. "I gotta take a piss."

"So take one," Johnny says.

"Can I go behind a tree or something'?"

"Take it here," growls Johnny. "Or piss in your pants."

"Ah, come on, Johnny," I say. "I don't want to take a piss in front of you."

"Why not?" Johnny says. "I seen what you got before, McNeil. It ain't nothin' special."

I'm thinking I can go behind a tree and run far enough to get away from him, but Johnny figures out what I'm planning. I give up on it. It's probably too dangerous anyway — Johnny's a crack shot and quick on the trigger. But I do have to piss. That much is true. I stop and pull my cock out. Steam billows from the ground and old leaves and needles where I piss. I shake off, shove my cock back into my pants, and zip up.

Johnny pokes the bore of the gun into my back. "Keep moving," he says. I do. We walk for five minutes without talking. We are far enough into the woods now that he can shoot me and even Charlie probably won't hear the shot.

"Johnny," I say. "I —"

"Shut the fuck up, McNeil," Johnny says. "You talk too much."

There is a turn in the path, around a deadfall I remember from years of coming back here hunting with Johnny. Up beyond it, once the path swings back on track, is a swamp, and then a clearing. Johnny is gonna shoot me there and chuck me in the swamp. No Husqvarna treatment for me. Johnny must think the swamp is safer. He is right. Once the swamp gets me, he might get lucky and no one will ever find my body.

AT SIX O'CLOCK MOM GOES up to Irene's and asks Tom to drive her into town to look for Jake. "If he comes while I'm gone you make him stay," she tells me. "Don't you let him go 'til I get back, you hear?"

"I hear," I say.

I kind of hope Jake comes while she is gone. Mom tells me to get my own dinner out the fridge, but there's nothing in there — there never is the last week before cheque day — so I have some crackers with peanut butter and a glass of milk and watch *M*A*S*H* on TV. I think about going up to Irene's for a visit but Mom will kill me if she comes home and I'm not here. And I don't want to miss Jake. So I lie down on the couch and fall asleep. I dream I'm in the woods with Jake and we are running from something, some bellowing monster who is knocking over trees and screaming and breathing purple smoke in the air and making it hard to see. Jake has my hand and we're running and Jake keeps saying, over and over again, "We came from the earth and we shall go back into the earth."

I don't know what it means and it feels like it's getting harder to hold on to Jake's hand. The air is getting darker with that purple smoke and I know the monster is getting closer though

I can only hear him and not see him and Jake's hand is hot and sweaty and starting to slip out of mine. Jake is thinking that when the purple smoke runs out the monster will stop but I want to tell him this isn't true. The monster will keep on coming, purple smoke or not. The monster is not really mad at Jake. The monster is just being a monster and Jake is in his way.

I wake up scared and almost crying for some reason and Mom still isn't home. I turn on the TV and watch *Three's Company* and wait for Jake and try to forget the purple air and the monster and laugh at Jack, Terri, Janet, Larry and Mr. Furley.

I can't, though.

I should always listen to my dreams, 'cause sometimes they turn out to be realer than television.

JUST AROUND THE BEND A tall, crooked black spruce is leaning into the path. It's bright green and dripping rain, one of those that in winter will be so heavy with snow the branches'll sag under the weight and you'll have to step off the path altogether and go around if you don't want all that snow to come avalanching down on your head when you pass. I don't remember this tree being here, though by the looks of it, it's ten years old. I know all about trees from the years I spent at the mill, and the winter I spent up north with the silviculture crew. That was a good winter, and being in the woods, even having Johnny with a twelve-gauge shotgun at my back, reminds me of it.

"Rejoice with trembling!" Johnny says suddenly, out of nowhere, and laughs.

Of all the things Johnny has said so far, this is the strangest, and I feel a goose walk across my grave. I think how soon it might be that that grave is dug — if Johnny even bothers and doesn't just throw me into the swamp to be sucked into the earth like a stone. The acid must be working in him good, because it doesn't even *sound* like him, and it makes no sense either. I don't want to know what's going on in his head, and I don't turn around because I know he'll be looking at me and I don't want to see him smile.

I realize I shouldn't go around the spruce like Johnny expects. The idea comes to me all at once, and just in time. Up ahead is the clearing, and the swamp, and the hunting blind me and Johnny built all those summers ago and had to clear of the dead branches covered with rusted needles and then cover in strips of new spruce to hide us from the deer. It's funny how you know some things, even when no one tells you — Johnny is gonna stand in that blind when he shoots me and I can almost hear how the shot will echo up through the trees, and see Johnny standing there breathing heavy while I lie bleeding in the middle of the swamp and sinking all night into the water and muck.

"We come from the earth and so we shall return to the earth," I hear my father say in my head, from one of his Sunday sermons, and for a minute, before I walk into the spruce, it is as if *I* done the purple microdot. Things are so intense and the trees around me so distinct and the sound of Johnny breathing and I can see him, though he is behind, bringing the shotgun to my head, as if he is practising. And then I walk into the branches of the tree and push through them hard like I am gonna force myself the whole way past the tree into the path beyond.

Rejoice with trembling, Johnny said.

I hope so, for mine and Nathan and even Johnny's sake, and when I sense he has stepped into the space behind me, in range of the branches, I let them lash back into his face and spring to one side.

"Fuck!" Johnny cries, and the gun goes off. For a minute I think I have been shot and am looking down. I can see Johnny below me dancing from where the spruce branches have lashed him in the face, and holding on to his eye, the gun pointing harmlessly to the ground. The shot is so close my ears are still ringing with it, but I run through the woods. I think of Johnny's phrase — *rejoice with trembling*. The trees sail by and Johnny shouts, "McNeil!" He curses and screams and tries to reload the gun. I run farther into the woods, farther than I have ever been even when Johnny and I were hunting. I can't hear anything behind me, but I keep going, like somehow, in all the vastness of this land and the pointlessness of its anger and the certainty of its vengeance and the way the land and the people suck you into the swamp of its hopelessness I can somehow still come through to the other side, to get what I came for, Nathan, and the two of us can leave this goddamned fucking place forever.

JAKE TRIED TO WRITE A book once. He worked at it every night after work at the kitchen table on loose leaf and when Mom asked to read it he said she would have to wait 'til it was finished. I was seven then and I could read, and I knew Jake hid the book in the bedroom closet in a shoebox and Mom didn't know it was there. So one day when Mom and Jake weren't home I went and found it and tried to read some of it. There were some big words I didn't know, but I found out Jake knew this girl named Cindy in high school and they drank a "pint of lemon gin" together and then he got "laid." I didn't know what any of it meant, except Jake wrote he and Cindy were lying together in the field behind the North River Fire Hall after the Friday Night Junior dance and Jake asked her if she thought there was life on other planets when they were looking up at the stars.

"There's hardly life on this one," Cindy said.

I was still trying to figure this out when Mom came home and I didn't get it put back quick enough. She caught me in the closet and swore she'd beat me within an inch of my life if I didn't tell her what I was doing, and so I had to show her Jake's book. Then she wasn't mad anymore and she took it out to the kitchen and sat down at the table to read it. By the time Jake got home she was fit to be tied. She held up the papers to him.

"You slept with that slut Cindy Luxton?" she said.

"Where you'd get that?" Jake said.

"Nathan found it in the closet. Now answer me. You slept with that whore?"

Jake just got home from work, and he looked tired. He shrugged. "Eleven years ago," he said. "I was just telling my life story."

"If that's all the story you got," Mom said, "you ain't got much. Half the boys in town laid with that bitch."

"So what?" said Jake. "She was my first. I didn't care if she was somebody else's seconds. I was just writing."

"Burn it," said my mother. "You wanna live in this house with me, I ain't having you telling all and sundry who you laid down in a field with. I'm surprised you didn't get the clap."

"Jesus, Carla," Jake said. "That was four fucking years before I even *met* you."

"I don't care," said my mom. "Burn it, or get out."

Jake looked at me, and then back at the papers in Mom's hand. I stood in the doorway to the living room and watched them both. Jake took the papers, went outside and burnt them in the fireplace. I went out with him. "I'm sorry, Jake," I said, as we watched the papers burn.

"Don't worry about it, squirt."

"What's lemon gin, Jake?"

Jake didn't turn away from where he was watching the papers on fire. "That night? The sweetest thing I ever tasted."

"Who's Cindy Luxton, Jake?"

"That night? The sweetest person I ever met."

I didn't understand this either, and we watched the papers burn until they fell to ash and went out.

I RUN FOR HOURS, IT seems like, and when I stop I have a stitch in my side. I am drenched in sweat. Johnny is gone. The woods are dead quiet. I crouch down on the ground with my back against a tree. Johnny didn't let me bring my jacket — maybe he wants to keep it as a trophy — and I am getting colder. I try to keep warm by hugging my knees and rocking back and forth on my haunches while I keep an eye out for Johnny.

I think about what I should do.

I don't know where I am. I ran so hard and so fast I didn't bother to mark the way. The woods here are big. Go west and you can walk sixty miles all the way into Digby County and not cross so much as a logging road. To the north is Middlebridge, but that is five miles or more, and to the east lies Johnny and his gun. That leaves south, across the river and back out to Highway #7. I'll have to leave the Pinto at Johnny's place and worry about picking it up later, if Johnny ever comes down from the acid.

I START WALKING SOUTH, RUNNING over in my mind all the names of trees I ever knew in order to stop thinking about the possibility of running smack dab into Johnny. Hoptree, dogwood, ash, basswood, Douglas fir, beech, hemlock, buckthorn, cherry, plum, crabapple, tamarack, elder, elm, witch hazel, hackberry, chestnut, hickory, laurel, birch, madrone, honey locust, maple, oak, pawpaw, poplar, larch, ironwood, redbud, sumac, sycamore, tupelo, mulberry, viburnum, alder, willow, juniper, blue-beech, pine, spruce, yew, coffee tree and hackmatack.

It's strange — all those years of hunting deer in here only to be hunted myself, by a man I once considered my friend now stoned out of his mind on purple microdot with double-aught buckshot loaded into the breech of his gun and nothing short of murder on his mind.

I don't doubt it is double-aught shot, though it's illegal to own.

I know Johnny has some, and he would consider killing somebody with anything less to be cheesy and unprofessional. The crazy bastard once shot a rabbit with some out behind his house, and when we went to pick it up there was nothing left but the ears and the tail. "Imagine what that would do to a deer, or a person," he told me that day. "Fuckin' mincemeat, McNeil."

Fucking mincemeat.

If I ever get out of here, that can be my nickname.

Mincemeat McNeil. It has a nice ring to it.

I MAKE IT ALL THE way through woods, 'til I get to the river, without seeing Johnny. Memragouche bends to the east a mile and a half below the Eight-Mile Bridge and then bends back to the west before Johnny's. Below that is Great Falls, where Cleve Ramey built his wooden ramps every year and dipped gaspereau for the market in Japan. When we were kids we used to help him dip on Sunday for a quarter a crate. Sometimes we'd come home with two dollars or more, which we'd spend at Douglas's on Monday. My father didn't like Cleve, because he didn't go to church and he didn't wash and he exploited us boys from the village by making us work on Sunday when his regular crew wanted a day off. But we didn't mind. Once, when the planks on the ramp were soaked with foam from the river and treacherous, I slid off into the falls but Cleve happened to be walking the ramp, a rare thing. He grabbed me by the collar and dragged me back out again.

"Careful there, young fella," he said, reeking of pipe tobacco and sweat and fried fish, which his wife made him every morning for breakfast. "You go into those falls and you ain't gonna live to tell the tale."

I loved dipping fish with Cleve, even besides the money.

There was something about dipping a long pole into the falls and coming up with a netful of wriggling silver-sided fish. We'd dump them into the blue plastic crates and watch them flop and fight for breath, mouths gasping and eyes turning milk-blue as the life slowly drained out of them. Some of the men Cleve hired would wait until the crates were filled with fish then lug them back to the shore and dump them in bigger wooden crates on the truck. Cleve was too fat to dip, so he sat in a chair on the back of his truck and smoked his pipe and watched the dipping and kept a running tally of the crates being brought in from the ramps. Dad said he likely cheated us, but I didn't know it if he did. I kept track of my own crates, and the number Cleve wrote down on his tally sheet at the end of the day always matched mine.

When I reach the falls through the woods, I stop because it is like I can almost see those days again. Sometimes this happens in North River. I run across some place I'd been when I was a kid and the feeling of being back there is so strong it's like there's two places — the one now pasted on top of the one then. When this happens, and I remember something about being a kid, like how good it was to be dipping fish for Cleve when I was fourteen and how grown-up I felt having all that responsibility and money, it's like this great empty space opens up inside me I didn't even know was there. I almost feel like I want to cry.

It's weird. Here I am, running from Johnny and soaked right through and coming out of the trees to the banks and the white-water roar of the falls and no one but Johnny and his gun for miles around and I feel this way. Cleve Ramey has been dead for years — heart attack — and they tore down those dipping ramps ages ago. The gaspereau don't run like they used to. Acid rain from the States and Ontario has put paid to that. Same with the salmon. Only thing left that runs like it used to is river eels, and even the Japanese got a limit on how many of those they'll take. But damned if I don't have one of those moments right then, when I can almost see us all again, and I picture the ramps out over the water, and hear the shouting and laughing and old Cleve calling to his oldest son from his lawn chair on the back of his truck, "Get them goddamned crates out there, Aubrey! The boys *need* 'em!"

For a minute I forget all about Nathan, and Johnny and his gun. All I can remember is the past, swirling up and around and across and over me like water, drowning me in memory.

EVERY SPRING WHEN HE WAS home Jake would take me up to the top of Harmony Lake Road in spring near the river to smash June bugs with badminton rackets. They made a loud "pop" when we hit them and we smacked the bugs right out of the air. Jake kept score and I always won. Once I killed forty-two June bugs in one night. I asked Jake once if it wasn't a sin to murder June bugs.

"Naw," said Jake. "They don't feel. No bug feels."

I wondered sometimes though.

Sometimes I wondered if everything didn't feel.

But we did it anyway, because Jake said it was something he used to do when he was a kid at his house in Middlebridge and I liked to do things with Jake that he used to do when he was a kid. Like go with him to the North River fair in September and get on the Ferris wheel and look out over everything from way up high. Sometimes the wheel stopped with us on top and the chair rocked back and forth and I was scared. But Jake said not to be.

"It's safe, squirt," he said. "Just enjoy the view."

I told Jake it didn't look like North River at all.

"My old man always said when he took me up here when I

was a kid that it was a 'God's eye view.'"

"What's that mean, Jake?"

Jake laughed. "You know what, squirt? I have no idea."

That was the same month Mom made Jake burn his papers, and though we were up high and at the fair and Jake would get me cotton candy after I was sad. I could tell Jake was getting ready to leave, even though he never said anything to Mom or to me, and I was wondering if it wouldn't be for good. I almost asked him, but the Ferris wheel started again and we were spun back to the ground.

I START TO WALK DOWN along the river towards the eddies below the falls. If it was summer and the river was low I could have made it all the way across on the rocks at practically any point above or below without getting so much as a wet sneaker. But in August the water starts to rise, and by late September, after the fall rains, the river runs fast and wide and unbroken from Memragouche Lake to the ocean twenty miles away in Oldsport. The water is colder and the current swifter than she looks. I need to be careful where I step in. I think if I can get across the river here I can get out to the Highway #7 and hitch or walk to Carla's. I don't give thought to what will happen when I get there, or how I'm supposed to get back to the city without the Pinto.

Below the second eddy is a place they call the salmon pool, where the salmon spawned before the acid rain killed them off, where the out-of-town fisherman would line the banks with their fly rods every May and June hoping to catch a salmon griltz. Below that is the narrows, where the river pinches off to no more than a stone's throw across, and runs shallow over rocks and sand for a quarter mile before she deepens and broadens and ambles on her way again. I decide to cross here.

91

By the looks of it, the water isn't deep and I can get across no problem. I step in with my Nikes on. The water is freezing, and the current, even in these shallows, is strong, tugging at my legs and threatening to carry me off my feet and down the river if I'm not careful. For a moment when I first wade into the river, it feels like I'm above myself again, staring down, and suddenly I feel the fool. Why don't I face Johnny Lang anyway, instead of running off like a scared cat and ending up here, knee-deep and half-froze to death in the river? But Johnny has a gun, I tell myself, and I don't. Maybe in a fair fight I could take him. And even if I couldn't I would have the satisfaction of trying. But with Johnny there's no such thing as a fair fight. If I try, and get killed, what will happen to Nathan?

There's no such thing as heroes. Anyone who stands up to Johnny Lang has to be stupid. Most would end up dragging their chicken ass across the river in September 'cause they don't want to wind up dead. I wade further into the river, thinking this and that, and trying not to think about the water as it rises around me. I stop and gently place each foot ahead before I step, arms lifted to keep them dry, and so I won't lose my balance and go under. Then the bed of the river dips and the water reaches my nuts and the world turns blue for a minute. I gasp at the shock of it. The current pulls and pushes and is getting harder to fight. The river gurgles and murmurs and tugs seductively as it breaks around my waist, but I keep pushing on.

"Hey McNeil."

I don't bother to turn. There I am, standing in the middle of the river, my arms raised and water now up to my chest, and there's Johnny standing on the shore behind me. Maybe he had me in his sights all along and was waiting for me to wade into the river where I wouldn't be able to get away.

"Turn around," he says.

Slowly, a few steps at a time, I shuffle around against the current 'til I am facing Johnny, arms still raised like I am being held up in a cheesy Western. Johnny stands there on the bank, holding the gun loosely at his waist but pointing at me. He's smiling. "You're fucked, McNeil," he says. "I wasn't going to shoot you. Just scare you a little. But now I am."

"I know," I say, as Johnny slowly lifts the gun to his shoulder and aims it at my face. I close my eyes and wait for it. For whatever comes next. Let it be quick, I pray, though I don't believe in my father's God, or in any God at all. The shot comes. The explosion echoes up and down the river and suddenly I am under water and being carried away by the current and, for a while, in my confusion, I'm certain this is what death is, this cold swift numbness, this travelling towards something, God knows what, and the bittersweet milk-blue relief of not having to fight the current any longer.

MOM COMES BACK FROM TOWN at seven without Jake. She has a six-pack of beer under her arm. I don't know where she got the money and I don't ask. Maybe she borrowed it from Irene against what Jake was gonna give her. She opens one and sits down at the kitchen table. After a while she tells me to come and sit with her a bit.

"You remember when you was little, and me and Jake used to take turns doin' airplanes with you around the room?"

I nod. I remember once Mom was drinking and she dropped me and Jake yelled at her. She might have remembered too, for next she says, "You remember when you fell down and broke your collarbone, and Dr. Bell had to set it, and you wore a sling to school that year?"

"I remember."

Whenever Mom drinks she plays the remember game. It's like she's sad for things that happened a long time ago, though I don't remember things being any different than they are now except for missing Jake. But I like when Mom gets this way. Sometimes she calls me "hon" and ruffles my hair like Jake used to do. Sometimes, though, she cries, and I can't tell what she's crying about. And sometimes she gets mad and throws things, or just passes out in her bed when she's had enough. Tonight though she stops the remember game, looks at the clock above the sink, which says it's ten past seven, and then out the window.

"He ain't comin'," she says.

I know better than to say anything, though I think she's wrong.

"If he was comin'," she says, "he'd be here by now, wouldn't he?"

She looks at me, and I stay in my chair looking at her like I don't know what she's saying. "Never mind," she says. "Get me another beer from the fridge."

If Jake's coming, I think, he better hurry up, 'cause she's gonna be drunk as a skunk by the time he gets here. Mom makes me turn on the radio to CKBW, where they're playing the top ten country countdown, and she gets up and forces me to dance with her to Ricky Skaggs. After, she's winded and has to sit down. The Silver Fox is next, who Mom doesn't like. We sit and listen to the radio. Outside it starts raining again, and when the knock comes at the door we don't know who it could be. We didn't hear a car, so it can't be Jake, and Mom doesn't think it's Irene out in the rain and she doesn't come after dinner anyway. She tells me to get it and I open the door and there's Jake, soaked and shivering on the stoop with no Pinto behind him, and a bad scratch on his cheek and his wet hair plastered flat to his head and frowning a little like Jake always does.

"Heyya squirt," Jake says.

Part II

NORTH RIVER USED TO BE called Saakawachkik by the Indians. My father says the word means "old one," and North River is really named after a woman who used to live in the Mi'kmaq village who was a witch. When we were kids we used to go to the old village — we knew it as the Indian Gardens — and hunt for arrowheads along the banks of the Memragouche. Sometimes we even saw some real Indians there — an old man in galoshes from the Wildcat Reserve setting muskrat traps along the shore, or a younger man hunting bear or deer with his rifle on the reserve lands that bordered the gardens. Johnny Lang had some Indian blood in him from his mother's side, and he spent some time hunting on the reserve, and once or twice took me with him. He didn't introduce me to any of his friends on the reserve, though I knew he had some; we always stuck to the woods. Sometimes we'd see a carload of reserve boys in North River, shooting the drag on Saturday night or parked behind the Masonic Hall drinking and smoking joints. They were always in a beat-up station wagon or old van with rims and rocker panels painted with mud from the Reserve Road. Johnny called their cars "Injun Engines," though he was careful where and when he said it. Even Johnny Lang knew not to fuck with Wildcat Reserve boys.

MY FATHER WOULD NOT ADMIT it, but Johnny Lang wasn't the only one with Indian blood in him. My father's hair was raven black and his skin as brown as a chestnut. I found out later my grandmother, who wanted my father to become a preacher, was born on the reserve, though she was adopted into a white family in North River when she was very young and didn't admit to coming from Wildcat at all.

It was my grandfather who told me about it.

"Sure," he said to me, one Sunday afternoon in August when we were turning the hay over in the fields with pitchforks to let it dry. I was fifteen then, and I came out to work at the farm alongside my granddad as much as I could. "Your grandmother's as Injun as they come, and so is your father. You ain't never noticed?"

"None much," I say.

"Your grandmother don't like to talk about it, and I'll be a crossed goose if I ever held it against a woman where she come from or whose people she was born into. But she was raised white, which is what counts."

It wasn't long after I went with my father to the Sunday service on the reserve. Twice a month my father would go there and preach at the community hall on Sunday night, and most times he took me with him. Mostly old people came, and sat in the wooden chairs and listened to my father go on about the Lord Our God. An old Mi'kmaq woman sat beside me and whispered out of the corner of her mouth, "You the preacher's son?"

I nodded, and she said, "Your father come from here."

"From where?" I whispered back, though I already knew because of my grandfather. My father heard us talking and shot me a look from where he stood at his pulpit, which was a metal music stand where he kept his reading glasses and the papers for his sermon.

"From *here*," hissed the old woman. She didn't once look at me — she kept her eyes glued all the while on my father, who was telling us about Jesus coming to the river Jordan to be baptized by John. "Your father's part of us. That makes you part of us, too, though not as much a part as he is."

It made sense to me then, why they let my father preach twice a month at the Wildcat community hall. And why some of the old Mi'kmaq women like the one who sat beside me, Saakawachkik, half-smiled to themselves and lowered their eyes to the floor while he spoke of Jesus and salvation.

I WAS BORN ON A Sunday. I had blue eyes. Jake said the brightest things about me were my eyes. Mom said that proved Jake wasn't my father because he had brown eyes. But I heard Jake tell her once that his mother had blue eyes and I must have got them from her. I never met Jake's mother, but I can picture her sometimes.

JAKE COMES INTO THE HOUSE and I say, "Jake? Where's your leather?"

Jake looks at me and shrugs. Mom gets up from the table and I can see she's feeling her beer and I look at Jake and know he can see it too. "Hi Carla," he says.

"Hello Jake. You're a sight for sore eyes."

He is too. He's soaked through and through and his hair is sticking up and his eyes are red, like he's been drinking, or crying. Mom tells me to run in the bathroom and get Jake a towel. By the time I get out Jake is sitting down and Mom's staring at him like she's never seen him before. She keeps plucking at the lint on her slacks and shifting in her seat and taking sips of her beer. Jake isn't saying anything, just staring down at his hands folded on the table. I hand him the towel.

"Thanks, squirt," he says.

"You're welcome, Jake," I say and I watch as he starts drying off his face and hair.

"So what you been up to?" Mom says.

"You know," says Jake. "Working."

Jake lays the towel down on the table and Mom starts playing with the corner of it. I take a seat between them, though neither of them looks at me. Mom's looking at Jake and Jake's still staring at his hands. Outside the rain is falling harder. I can hear it drumming on the roofs of Jake's cars-on-blocks. That makes me think of something.

"Where's your Pinto, Jake?" I ask him.

"At Johnny Lang's," Jake says.

"What's it doing there?" asks Mom. Jake doesn't answer. Mom tells me to get another beer from the fridge.

"You want one, Jake?" I ask. Mom shoots me a look. Jake shakes his head. I get the beer from the fridge, open it, and take it to Mom and sit back down.

"I got something to say," Jake says.

"Say it," says Mom, and it's like something has passed between them while my back was turned. Mom doesn't look nervous around Jake anymore, and Jake looks like he's lost something or he doesn't know where he's at. I wonder if he's upset because of his leather. I wonder if it has something to do with my dream of Jake in the forest with the gun and the purple smoke.

"I want Nathan," Jake says.

For a minute I don't know what Jake is saying. But Mom acts like she knows. She takes a long drink of her beer, sets the bottle down, and squints hard at Jake.

"Over my dead body," she says.

"He's mine as much as yours," Jake says. "You've had him long enough."

"He ain't yours at all," Mom says. "You ain't got nothin' to do with him. He belongs to someone else."

Jake sighs. He looks really, really tired, like he used to when he'd come home Fridays from the mill in his dungarees, covered in sawdust and reeking of diesel. He'd fall asleep on the couch in the living room in front of the TV without changing.

"He's mine," Jake says. "You know it and I know it, and everyone else knows it too."

"You can't prove it," Mom says. "There ain't nothin' on his birth certificate. I told 'em I didn't know."

"There's tests," Jake says. "I can get one and prove it."

"And who's got the money for that?" Mom says.

"I got money," Jake says.

Mom takes another drink of her beer. "How much money you got, Jake?"

Jake looks at me, then back at Mom. "Send him out," he says. "We shouldn't be talking about this in front of him."

Mom looks at me. "Git," she says.

"But Jake —" I say, and Mom reaches out to hit me.

He reaches out and grabs her arm. "Don't you fucking dare."

"Fuck you!" Mom screams. "Fuck you, Mister Jake fuckin' hotshot McNeil."

"Git," Jake says, and I get up and run into my room while Mom is screaming at Jake.

I LIE IN MY ROOM on the bed and listen to them. It's like the world is hanging between them, and what they say. That's how hard I listen. I keep my light off, 'cause it feels like I can listen better that way. Sometimes Mom screams and shouts and sometimes she gets quiet and Jake talks low and I can barely hear him. And sometimes they say nothing at all. I strain in the darkness for some sound, for some whisper of what they are saying and where they are going and what Jake's planning to do.

Dear God, I whisper to myself. Please let Jake win.

WE FIGHT FOR HOURS, IT seems like, and I'm already so tired from my run-in with Johnny Lang. I crawled from the river an eighth of a mile below the narrows. It was a miracle I didn't drown. It was even more of a miracle that somehow, even at that range with the double-aught shot, Johnny had missed. My legs and arms were bruised up from being tossed on the rocks, and I had to walk an hour to Carla's but by the time I got here I thought I was ready for this, that for the last six months I had been getting ready for this, but Carla is tough. Nothing is ever so hard as fighting with someone you used to love.

BROWN EYES. BLUE EYES. BROWN eyes. Blue eyes. Once when I was real little Jake put me on his shoulders and I asked him to go in the bathroom so I could see us in the mirror like that. He stood way back and I looked at me sitting up there on top of him and the two of us like one person glued together. I laughed and Jake smiled and I asked him if he saw our eyes.

Brown eyes. Blue eyes. Brown eyes. Blue eyes.

"I see 'em," Jake said.

"How come we got different eyes, Jake?"

"Brown eyes, blue eyes," Jake said. "Not really that much different."

"What colour is Mom's eyes, Jake?"

Jake stopped smiling a little. "They change," he said. "Depending on the day."

"DON'T YOU FUCKIN' TELL ME what I'm supposed to do with him and how I treat 'im. He ain't yours to tell anything, and I'm not yours to tell anything to either, you goddamned no-good-for-nothing son-of-a-fuckin'-bitch! You're the one who took off to Halifax and left us here with nothin' but a pot to piss in. Big man! Big fuckin' man. And who's comin' slinkin' back now lookin' for favours and lookin' to take 'im away? No way, Mister man. Mister smart-fuckin'-alec-Jake-fuckhead-McNeil. Not me. Not Nathan. You can take whatever you brought with you and stuff it up your fuckin' ass for all I care. You hear me? You goddamned well hear me, you bastard? Up your god-damned faggot fuckin' ass!"

I TAKE OFF MY CLOTHES and fall asleep. When I wake up I see Mom standing over my bed with the light from the living-room lamp shining through the bedroom door. She's breathing hard and she stinks of beer. "Get up," she says. The house is silent. Jake must be gone. "Get up," Mom says. "I'm not tellin' you again."

I get out of bed like she asks and go to put on my jeans. "Never mind those," she says.

"I only got my underwear," I tell her.

"I said never mind," Mom says. "Get out there."

I go into the living room and Mom pushes me towards the kitchen. I'm surprised to see Jake still here. He's sitting at the kitchen table looking out the window. I stand in the middle of the kitchen floor. The stove has gone out and the linoleum is freezing the bottom of my feet. I'm hugging myself and shivering. Jake looks at me. "Jesus, Carla. He ain't got no clothes on."

"There," Mom says, pushing me hard towards Jake. I stumble and fall to the floor.

Jake jumps up. "Stop it!" he says. "You stop it right now!"

"You want 'im," Mom says. "You take 'im."

"Where's his fucking clothes?"

I lie on the floor, still shivering, looking up at Jake. Then Mom kicks me hard in the ribs with her shoe. I cry out and Jake lunges over me at her and I scramble under the table to get away from them, my side aching from where she booted me. I turn and watch as Jake puts his hands around Mom's throat and pushes her up against the fridge. Mom's face is turning purple and Jake is screaming.

"You leave him the fuck alone, you hear me? You leave him the fuck alone!"

I think he's gonna kill her, and go to jail, but he lets go. Mom bends over coughing and sputtering and holding on to her throat. "You bastard," she croaks.

Jake turns to me under the table. "Go get your clothes on," he says.

"You fucking bastard," Mom whispers, trying to stand up straight.

Jake reaches into the back pocket of his jeans and brings out his wallet. He takes out money, more money than I've ever seen, and holds it out to Mom. "Here," he says. "Like we said. You take this for Nathan, and I'll keep sending you more. The services don't even have to know he's gone. But you don't let me take him, and I'm calling them. I'll do everything I can to make sure he gets taken away from you." Mom doesn't say nothing. She's still rubbing her throat but she's also looking at the money Jake is holding out to her.

"How much?" she says.

"One thousand," Jake says. "All I got, except what I need to live."

"When you want him?"

"Tonight," Jake says.

Mom looks past Jake at me crouched under the table, staring

out at them like I'm in a cage. "You go get some clothes on," she says.

I crawl out from under the table and stand up, careful 'cause it hurts my ribs when I move and take a breath. I watch in case she comes at me again. But Jake is standing between me and her.

"Where are you taking him?" she asks.

"To the city," Jake answers.

"They won't let you keep him."

"Who won't?"

"The services in there. You're not fit. Who's gonna look after him while you're at work? Who's gonna cook for him? And get his clothes? You can't take care of him. Someone will take him away, or you'll get tired of him and bring him back."

But as Mom is talking she takes the money from Jake and folds it up and puts it away in her jeans. She sees me standing and watching. "Go on," she says. "Git."

I run through the living room into my bedroom and get dressed in the dark. Mom keeps talking real loud at Jake. "You keep that money coming," she says, "or I'll tell the services why you want him."

"And why's that?" Jake says.

"To have at him," Mom says. "I'll tell the services that and they'll bring him home faster than lightning and put you in jail."

"You'd be lying," Jake says.

"Who'd know that?" Mom says. "I'll tell 'em you been at Nathan since he was little. That you're at him all the time and I can't stop you."

"Nathan will tell the truth," Jake says.

"No one believes eight-year-old kids," Mom says. "Especially about that. They'll think he's protecting you, or hiding what he and you done."

"You try that," Jake says, "and I'll kill you."

Mom laughs. "You? You don't have it in you, Jake McNeil. Anyway. You keep that money coming and I'll let you have him for a bit. Not forever, mind you, but for a bit."

"Nathan!" Jake hollers. "Come on!"

I am dressed, with my sneakers tied and my jacket on. I come out into the kitchen. Mom's sitting down now with another beer. Jake is standing by the door, waiting. Mom looks at me. She looks wild and drunk-sick. "Don't you get nothing on your mind about staying for good," she says. "You'll be coming back."

"Come on," Jake says and opens the door. It's not raining anymore and the sky has cleared. Through the open door I see tiny yellow stars shining above the trees in the woods past the yard.

We leave. "There's the moon," I say to Jake when we get out into the road and start walking up towards the river. Jake looks at it, hanging over the tops of the trees. He takes my hand as we walk but says nothing.

"Where we going?" I ask, but he doesn't say nothing to that either.

So I look up at the stars and at the moon, like I sometimes did when I was coming home late from Cub Scouts at North River Community Hall on Tuesdays.

The tiny yellow stars. The moon.

MY OLD MAN LIVES IN the Baptist Parsonage on the other side of the river. His church is in Middlebridge, four miles outside North River town limits, and the parsonage I lived in growing up was built in 1948 when the old parsonage burnt down and the bachelor minister got caught and died in the fire. It's a drafty old place, poorly built, with wood stoves in the parlour and kitchen and vents in the ceiling to let the heat up. When I was a kid and my parents had company I would lie over the vents in the hallway outside my room and listen to them play games in the kitchen. The Baptists in Middlebridge didn't go in for cards or dice, so the games my parents played with their parishioners had to be without. Sometimes they played charades — my father made them up beforehand and most of them were names or stories from the New Testament — and sometimes they just talked about people in the village. My mother used to joke that being a minister was the only job in the world where gossiping about the neighbours was a duty and not a sin.

My father laughed at this. Before she died he laughed a lot more than he did after. I blamed God when my mother died and stopped praying, and my father blamed the world and stopped laughing.

WE COME TO THE BRIDGE and the stars are spinning halfway across the North River sky. Jake holds my hand in his. The moon is like a pale rider above the tops of the trees 'til a cloud drifts over it. I want to say, "Can you hear me, moon?" but the moon won't answer.

Jake squeezes my hand as we walk across the bridge.

I would be scared of the bridge in the dark if Jake wasn't with me.

AFTER AN HOUR OF WALKING we come to Eight-Mile Bridge. Nathan squeezes my hand tight, like he's scared, just as the moon is crossed by a silver-grey cloud. I squeeze back and say, "Come on, squirt."

I still don't tell him where we're going, though I guess he probably knows by now. My father usually goes to bed by nine or so, and I hope he'll hear the knock at the door this late. I decide if he doesn't we'll sleep in the garage until morning.

When we're halfway across the bridge, the moon comes out again and I can see the gabled roof of the parsonage thrusting up over the tops of the trees past the bend in the river. Beyond stands the squat wooden steeple of the Baptist church. Middle-bridge is pretty compared to North River. Around the church-yard and the parsonage some soldier planted red maples after coming home from the Second World War. My mother loved those trees, and wouldn't let us climb them when we were young, though because of their smooth thick grey branches starting just a few feet from the ground we sometimes climbed them anyway.

"We're going to your house?" Nathan says, and I can hear something in his voice. He's never been to the parsonage, though once or twice when we were fishing for trout below the bridge at Granddad's hole I pointed it out to him. "Your father lives there?" he asks me now.

Your grandfather, I almost say, then stop. Why bother? Nathan's never seen him, even in a place as small as North River. Neither of them knows what the other looks like. We get off the bridge and turn onto Church Road. The lights in all the houses are out, though it isn't much past ten, and except for some dog barking up the road it's quiet. It feels so lonesome: Nathan and I, walking down the road hand in hand past those dark silent houses with everyone asleep. It's like we are stealing back into something, or coming from somewhere far away.

JAKE SAYS THE WAY YOU become a man is to start acting like one. I ask Jake on the way to his father's house if he thought I could soon be a man, or would I have to wait a bit longer. "What makes you think of that?" Jake says.

"I don't know," I say. "I'm almost nine now. Mom says that's old enough to do some things."

"Like?" Jake says.

"Wash the dishes. Sweep the floor. Go by myself to the store to buy milk and bread when we need it."

"That isn't man's stuff," says Jake. "That's woman's stuff."

"What's man's stuff then?"

Jake doesn't answer right off. "I don't know," he says finally. "Working a good job, I guess. Cutting trees or something, or fixing the car or hunting and fishing."

"I hunt and fish, Jake," I say. "You've taken me hunting and fishing lots a times."

"And girls," Jake says. "Girls are man stuff. You like any girls yet?"

I think of the girls in my class in Grade Three. "Melanie Winters has blond hair," I tell Jake. "And she sometimes gives me her apple when she don't want it at recess."

Jake squeezes my hand again. "That's man stuff," Jake says.

"Do you like any girls, Jake?"

Once upon a time, Jake liked Mom. I remember when I was little they used to hug and stuff on the couch at night in front of the TV, and I used to sometimes sit all warm between them before I went to bed.

"I haven't got time for girls," Jake says. "Girls ain't nothing but trouble anyway."

I want to ask Jake how girls could be man's stuff, and he was a man, and they are nothing but trouble anyway. But I don't. Sometimes I can tell when Jake is getting tired of talking. Besides, we're almost at his father's place.

"You wait here," Jake says when we reach the drive to the house. I say yes, and stand and wait for Jake while he goes up to the side door and knocks. Before long a light comes on in a window upstairs, then another light downstairs. The door Jake is standing in front of opens, and I can hear a voice speaking to Jake, though I can't make out what they are saying.

I stand there a long while, it seems, and watch Jake standing on the front step talking to his father, who I can't see 'cause he's in the house. Soon Jake's father sticks his head out the door and looks down the driveway at me, but I can't see him clear either because the light above the steps where Jake is standing is too bright. So I stand there and look up and down the road at all the other houses in Middlebridge.

"JAKE," DAD SAYS. HE'S BLINKING at me in his robe and bare feet, his hair stuck up and sleep welts running up and down one side of his face. He looks as if he thinks he might still be dreaming. "What are you doing here?"

"I need a place," I tell him.

"Now? I didn't even know you were in North River."

"I got in today," I tell him.

He looks past my shoulder into the driveway. "Where's your car?"

"It's a long story."

"Come on in." He yawns.

"Nathan's with me."

Dad stops yawning. "Where's his mother?"

"Home."

"Why isn't he with her?"

"'Cause," I tell him, looking him straight in the eye. "I took him from her."

He looks down and around, like I might be hiding Nathan under the steps.

"Where is he?"

"He's by the road," I say. "I wanted to check to see if it was okay first."

Dad leans his head out of the doorway to look at Nathan, who's standing out under the street light, watching at us. Then Dad pulls back. "Why did you take him?"

"Because," I say. "She's no good for him."

"And you are?"

"Better than she is."

He looks at me in the old way, the way I remember when I lived here and he thought I was doing something wrong or stupid. "It can't be legal," he says, "to up and take a boy from his mother, no matter how good or bad she is for him. There are laws, Jake. Did you take any of those into account before you hauled off and did this?"

"I thought about 'em," I say.

"Them, not 'em," says my father.

"I thought about *them*," I say. "I told Carla I'd pay her to keep away from Nathan."

"You *bought* him from her?"

I shrug. "It's like ... what do they call that, when you pay the wife to take the kids after a breakup?"

"Child support," says Dad.

"It's like that," I say. "Only backwards."

"That's silly," says my father. "You and Carla weren't married."

"It's late. Nathan's cold, and so am I. Can we come in?"

"Where's your jacket?"

"Long —"

"— story," Dad finishes, shaking his head. "I know. Same as everything with you. The longest story I know, Jacob, is the Bible and there's always been an abiding interest in hearing that."

122

I want to ask him what the fucking Bible has to do with any-thing, me without a jacket and with an eight-year-old standing by himself on the side of the road freezing to death. But if there is one thing you don't question my father on, it's preaching. Not if you want in the man's house, that is. I wait. He looks at me — that same disgusted, tired look again — and then sighs and holds wide the door.

"Come in, then," he says. "I've got services tomorrow, and this isn't helping any."

"Nathan!" I shout and wave. "Come on."

Nathan runs up the driveway and stops when he gets to the steps and the doorway and me. He stands behind me and looks up shyly at his grandfather.

"Nathan," I say. "Meet Dad. Dad. Meet Nathan."

I see something pass across the old man's face when he sees Nathan up close for the first time. It's like a shock, or a pain, that flickers there for a second and then just as quick is gone.

I HAVEN'T BEEN IN DAD'S house for six months, ever since I left for Halifax. I stayed there sometimes when I lived in North River, when Carla didn't want me staying with her and I didn't think I could handle Johnny and Charlie for any amount of time. Nothing is different. The kitchen is the same as it was when my mother died. She complained the cupboards were too high — built for giants, she said — and Dad promised to speak to the church elders about getting them lowered or replaced. But after she died he didn't bother. What was the use? He was tall enough to reach them. But he kept the wooden step stool she used to reach the dishes on higher shelves. It was sitting under the windowsill beside the table. Every time I came in I looked at it. She fell off it once, not long after she started chemo and her hair was falling out and she was really sick but trying to make him lunch anyway. Dad came home at noon from the church rectory and found her lying on the linoleum floor in front of the cupboards, burning up with fever and asleep where she'd fallen. He picked her up and carried her upstairs to bed.

"She's so light," he told me when I got home from school. "She doesn't weigh anything at all."

124

That was the first time I'd seen Dad cry since we found out Mom had cancer.

He looks at me now, looking at the stool. "You hungry?" he asks.

I look at Nathan. Nathan nods. "I'll get us a sandwich or something outta the fridge," I say.

"Good," Dad says. "I'm going back to bed. You can sleep in your old room. And Nathan can sleep down here on the daybed."

The daybed is a small room off the kitchen behind the stove, which my mother used as a pantry. It has an iron cot taking up one side, but my mother called it "the daybed" and so we did too. There's also another room upstairs, but he didn't suggest I put Nathan there. It was my sister Ruth's room, who died when she was three.

"Okay," I say. "The daybed's good."

"All right," he says. "'Night."

"'Night," I say.

"'Night," says Nathan.

Dad looks at him once more, and I see that look pass across his face again. Then he's gone. Nathan and I listen to the creak of him passing up the stairs and crossing the floorboards in the upstairs hallway. When it's quiet I start rooting in the fridge for something to make sandwiches.

"It's a big house, isn't it, Jake?"

"What, this house?"

"Yeah," says Nathan. "Bigger'n ours, isn't it?"

The parsonage isn't that big — the kitchen, the parlour, my father's study and the tiny room on the lower floor, three bedrooms and a bathroom on the upper. There's half an attic, and a root cellar with a wooden vegetable bin and hot water tank, and that's about it. But compared to what Nathan's used to, I suppose it's big. "Take your jacket off," I tell him. "It's warm enough without it."

Nathan does as he is told, and I get out some sliced ham for sandwiches. I make them with butter and mustard on Ben's bread and Nathan asks me a thousand and one questions about the house and my father. "He's real tall, isn't he, Jake? He's got a moustache. Which side of the house is your bedroom on? Did you ever shut out all the lights and play hide and seek? Your father got a dog? Did you think the house could fall into the river, 'cause it's so close, if the water ever gets high?" Do you, do you, do you, did you.

I give Nathan his sandwich and a glass of milk from a pail in the fridge. Nathan doesn't want to drink the milk, because it's yellow. "It's fresh," I say. "Brian Fancy keeps dairy cows and gives it to Dad every week."

"You mean it comes from a cow and not from a carton?"

"All milk comes from a cow, Nathan. It's a matter of who gets their hands on it after it comes out and what they do with it."

"What about sheep? Do sheep have milk?"

"All animals have milk. We just don't drink some of it."

"Why not?"

"'Cause some of it doesn't taste good."

"Oh," says Nathan.

He is full of questions. I'm worn out with them after ten minutes. I tell him to hurry up and finish his sandwich so he can go to bed. He does, but he won't touch the milk. I drink it for him, and take him into the daybed. He sits on the edge of the bed and undresses, still chattering away. I try to answer him the best I can. When he takes his shirt off I see the bruise starting on his ribcage where his mother kicked him.

"That hurt?" I ask.

"A little," Nathan says.

"Wait here," I tell him.

I creep upstairs, quiet so I won't wake Dad, and go into the bathroom. I find a tin of Rawleigh's Camphor Balm in the medicine cabinet that looks like it's been there since Jesus was in short pants and go back downstairs with it. Nathan's still sitting in his underwear on the edge of the bed, playing with the beads on the fringe of the lampshade on the table beside the cot. I twist off the cover, bend down, and spread it with two fingers over his bruise.

"It stinks," says Nathan.

"It'll help," I say. "You'll see. Now get in bed."

The cot squeaks as Nathan gets turned around and crawls under the covers. I feel an urge to bend over and kiss him on the cheek, but I don't. Instead I reach out and muss his hair on the pillow.

"'Night, kid," I say.

"'Night, Jake," Nathan answers. "I'm real glad you came back for me."

I stand up and reach out to turn out the lamp. Nathan's staring up at me, trusting me, counting on me. I feel scared then, more scared than when I thought Johnny was gonna kill me in the swamp. I turn out the light quick and leave the room, because I can't take him looking at me like that anymore.

I DREAM WE ARE IN a rowboat on the river. Jake's dad is standing in the front of the boat, facing the water. He's dressed in his black preacher clothes, reading out loud from his Bible. Jake is rowing in the middle and I am kneeling on the floor in the back facing Jake and scooping out the water with a bailing jar. Water is pouring in through the cracks in the boards.

"It's gonna sink, Jake," I tell him.

"Doesn't matter," says Jake. "We'll keep on rowing."

"We'll keep on praying!" shouts Jake's dad from the front of the boat.

Mom is standing on the shore, with Irene Lang and Wendy McNutt, who is holding baby Lucy in her arms. They are all smiling and waving at us, even Mom. On the other side of the river are Johnny Lang and Charlie Whynot. Johnny Lang is pointing a gun at us, and Charlie is trying to moonwalk along the shore. It starts to thunder, and I wake up in the dark without knowing where I am. Then I remember but my heart is still beating so loud in my ears from my dream I think for sure it will wake up Jake and his dad.

Not Jake's mom though. She is with baby Lucy. The memory

of her hangs over Jake's house like white smoke over the fields when they burn off the long grasses in July.

I DREAM I AM BACK in the woods again, being chased by Johnny. Carla is with me, and she is dragging Nathan behind her by the arm. "I'll say you were at him," Carla is saying, over and over again. "I'll say you were at him."

Then Carla turns into my father, and he says to me, "Jake, the longest story I know is the Bible, and we don't even know how it ends yet."

Then Johnny is right in front of me, like sometimes happens in dreams, and I am staring down the barrel of his gun. "Rejoice and tremble, McNeil," he tells me, and pulls the trigger.

I wake up in my old room, my heart pounding, the blast of the gun from my dream still echoing in my head. It's dark. A clock ticks from somewhere deep inside the house, and I wonder how Nathan is making out on the daybed. I think of going down to check on him, but I am too warm in my old bed. I must still be half asleep, because I think, "If dying feels like this, then I think I can handle it."

MY FATHER NAMED MY SISTER Ruth after the woman from the Bible, just as he named me Jacob, after he who wrestled with the angel. Ruth was two years younger than me and drowned in the river when I was five. I don't remember much about her, other than she had black hair and black eyes and she used to say "supercalifragilisticexpialidocious" from Mary Poppins and make everyone laugh. I have a vague memory of my mother lighting sparklers for us one New Year's Eve and Ruth running around in the snow in the side yard after dark with hers screaming "Sparkla! Spakla!" with the glow from it bathing her pudgy little face. I have another of her holding buttercups under all our chins to tell if we "liked buttah."

And that's all I remember about her, until she died.

She wandered out of the house one April afternoon when my mother was baking bread and fell into the river. They found her hours later, caught up in some dead wood. My mother died right there, my father said once, though it took another six years for the cancer to come and finish the job.

We didn't talk about Ruth when I was growing up. Once, when I was eleven, and my mother was at her sickest and the morphine wasn't doing anything for the pain, she shouted out

131

Ruth's name in the middle of the night. I lay in bed and listened to the river and shivered, though it was summer and the house was hot. It was like something dark with wings flew over the house that night, something cold without a name from one of my father's sermons, and I stayed still in case it decided to turn back and come for me.

The next morning, when my father got me breakfast before he went into his study, I asked him if he'd heard my mother call out Ruth's name.

"You were dreaming," he said.

But he didn't look at me when he said it, and I knew he'd heard it too. After supper my father brought my mother down to sit outside a half hour before bed. It took them twenty minutes to get down the stairs and outside to the armchair Dad set on the lawn. She stayed in her housecoat the whole time. She was so thin she hardly looked like my mother anymore. She sat and stared at the water with my father beside her in a lawn chair and me on the ground. I knew she was thinking about Ruth. My father brought out the radio and set it up on the lawn and we listened to the gospel station out of Trenton and the river flowed by, as swift and dark as wine.

IT WAS IN MY SISTER that the Indian came out full-blood in my family. She came out with a full head of raven black hair, my mother said, and dark eyes, and dark skin, with purple dimples at the tops of her thighs which my grandfather told me later was a sign of an Indian child.

My mother called Ruth "My Little Injun," though my father told her not to.

When I was seventeen and my father and I weren't getting along, I got up enough nerve to ask him about the Indian blood in our family.

"What Indian blood?" he said.

"Nana," I said. "And you. And Ruth."

"I don't know where you heard that," my father said, "but it's not true."

"Granddad says it is."

"Your grandfather says a lot of things I don't set much store by," my father said.

"What would be wrong with it, if it was true?" I said.

"Nothing," said my father. "But it isn't, so there's no need to bring it up."

I couldn't figure out what bothered my father so about it. It

133

wasn't that all Indians were heathens, because he preached to them and there were as many Christians on the reserve as in Middlebridge. And it wasn't because he was racist, because he always said the colour of a man's skin was created by God and therefore should be accepted. But it made my father small in my eyes. This one thing about him.

I was seventeen. Anything that made him small was welcome.

I WAS BORN ON A Saturday, my mother said, and my father was in his study, preparing his sermon for the Sunday morning service. The moon was full. It was a low-hanging moon, and I can imagine it there, a great orange-yellow wheel in the dark November sky above the river, with those lines carved deep into its ancient face that are supposed to be mountains and valleys and craters. My father sits at his desk, in an old grey sweater my mother knit him and a pair of faded jeans, writing out his sermon in longhand on a piece of foolscap, his face half-cast in shadow under the light of the green-shaded banker's lamp on the desk. Once my mother gathered up all my father's sermons and had them typed and printed up in a single, leather-bound book by a professional printer and gave it to him for a Christmas present. He kept the book in the glass breakfront in his study, and sometimes I went in and flipped through it 'til I found the one he was working on the day I was born, though he never got to deliver it because he was in the hospital with my mother.

"Jesus stood on Mount Olivet overlooking Jerusalem," my father wrote. He also wrote that Jesus said that just as a thief steals into a house during the night, so the owner of the house should like to know the thief is coming so that he can be prepared.

"And so it shall be with you when returns the Son of Man."

That never made any sense to me, that bit where Jesus says he will return like a thief in the night.

"Jake came like a thief in the night," my mother said to my father once about that sermon, the one he never gave.

"And Mount Olivet?" asked my father.

"Life," answered my mother. "Mount Olivet is life."

I must admit, I didn't understand this either.

THERE WAS A GREAT FIRE in Middlebridge, the one that burnt the first Baptist parsonage to the ground in 1947. That was the last year my granddad worked on the logging crews upriver, before he purchased the farm in Middlebridge and after he came home from the war. They lived in a rental house then, not far from the Wildcat Reserve where my grandmother was born and didn't admit to coming from. The fire started on the reserve, when a woman had a fight with her husband and went out and set the back woods afire in her rage. All the men on the reserve tried to put it out before it spread, but it had been a hot, dry summer and no matter what they did the fire kept burning, until most of them gave up, took their families and ran for the river, leaving their houses and horses and cattle and dogs to fend for themselves.

My grandfather was away at the logging camp, and they weren't due to run the logs down to North River for another week. My grandmother was alone with my five-year-old father. She was hanging the wash on the line when Bernadette Christmas, her closest neighbour who lived in the first house on the reserve-side, came running into the yard, her face soot-covered and sweating from working to put out the fire.

"You better git," she told my grandmother. "It's coming this way, and ain't nothing you or I or anyone can do to stop it."

My grandmother smelled the fire, of course, and saw the smoke billowing into the sky above the trees. But she thought the Indians had lit a bonfire, or someone was burning off the grasses in the fields. She thanked Bernadette and ran inside the house to get my father. By the time she came back out, Bernadette was gone. She could see the sky above the trees to the north was turning a deep crimson from the flames and the heat. Animals — deer and rabbit and skunks and fox and raccoons — were pouring out of the woods and running across her lawn. She saw a bear lumbering down the Reserve Road, away from the fire.

She hiked my father in her arms and started running down the Reserve Road. But it wasn't doing her any good. Already she could feel the heat from the fire and hear the unholy roar of it as it ate its way through the woods. She thought if she could get to the river she'd be safe, but the river was miles away, and she had a five-year-old to carry.

She turned back, towards the house.

"No, Mommy," cried my father. "Fire's coming!"

But my grandmother knew what she was doing. She took him and ran across the yard to the well. Already the first tendrils of flame were snaking out of the woods and slithering across the lawn, and the smoke was pouring thick and fast into the air and stinging her eyes. She set my father down on the grass and pushed the wooden cover off the top of the well. Then she picked up my father.

"Mommy," screamed my father. "Don't forget Bobby!"

My grandmother turned, and there was Bobby, my grandfather's blue tick hound, tied to a stump at the corner of the house. He was barking and choking himself from pulling at the end of the rope. She sat my father down and ran over and untied Bobby but he didn't go anywhere. He just kept barking.

"Mommy!" my father cried. "He's not running away!"

"Bobby'll be all right," said my grandmother.

She came back and looked down in the well. Perhaps if she'd been alone she could have tried to pick her way down the damp, slippery, moss-covered stones embedded into the sides of the shaft. Or she could have lowered the bucket from the hoist to the bottom and climbed down the rope. But she couldn't do either with my father in her arms. Suddenly a section of fire broke free of the woods. My grandmother felt a wall of heat behind her, and suddenly the oxygen was sucked from the air and she couldn't breathe. She could feel the back of her neck start to blister in the heat.

She did the only thing she could do.

She jumped, holding my father tightly in both arms. They dropped straight into the well, into the water at the bottom.

I WAKE UP WITH THE sun pouring in through the little window over my bed and the sound of the river in my ears. It's too early to get up — the house is quiet and I can tell Jake and his dad still aren't awake. And so I lie in the bed and look around at the room and try to stay real still and quiet. It's a nice room, with white wallpaper with little faded pink roses all over it. There is a desk, and an old lamp and a chest of drawers and a rocking chair and some old pictures of people I don't know on the wall. I wonder if one of them is Jake's mom.

There is a sound underneath the river, and the quiet of the house. A hum, the way the electric lines hum on certain days in the summer if you're out real early in the morning.

Irene Lang told me once Jesus is underneath everything, watching us.

I wonder if that hum is Jesus.

Or is Jesus the light, pouring in through the window beside the bed?

"SO," JAKE'S DAD SAYS. "WHAT'S all this about?"

"What's what all about?" says Jake.

"Don't play smart with me, Jacob. You know what I'm talking about. Coming here in the middle of the night with Nathan in tow. No car, no jacket. The boy's mother nowhere in sight. There must be more to this than you told me last night."

"No," says Jake. "I told you. That's it. I took him, and I'm taking him back to the city with me."

"When?"

"Today. If I can get there."

"What about your car?"

"It's at Johnny Lang's."

"And your jacket?"

"Same place."

"What's going on with you and Johnny Lang?"

"He tried to kill me."

"What?"

"He chased me through the woods with a shotgun and I got away."

"Why, for Lord's sake?"

"He was high. I don't know."

141

"I told you when you started hanging out with that boy years ago it would lead to trouble."

"You did."

"And hasn't it?"

"Yes."

"So, what are you gonna do?"

"I'm gonna go and get my car and Nathan and I are going back to the city."

"Are you taking him with you to get your car?"

"God no! What if something went wrong, or Johnny's still waiting for me?"

"Why don't you call the police?"

"Johnny really would kill me if I did that. I was kind of hoping he'd be calmed down by now, and I can get the car and leave."

"So. As I said. What are you doing with the boy while you're gone?"

"I was kind of hoping I could leave him here."

"I've got services this morning."

"He wouldn't go at nothing."

"I don't know, Jacob. I don't like leaving anyone here alone. You know that."

"Take him to church with you then. I'll be back for him in a couple hours, at the most."

"Who am I supposed to say he is, when my congregation asks why I got a seven-year-old boy in tow?"

"He's eight. And how about telling them the truth? They all know anyway."

"Do they?" Jake's father says. "Funny. Isn't one of them ever mentioned the fact to me."

"They know," Jake says. "Everyone in North River and Middlebridge knows everything about everyone."

"Maybe they do."

"Leave him here, then. Like I said. He won't go at nothing."

"Has he ever been to church?"

"I don't know. I don't think so."

"The boy is eight years old and he's never been to church?"

"Carla really isn't the church-going type."

"And what about you?

"You know the answer to that, don't you?"

"Sometimes," Jake's dad says, "I wonder what your mother would think about all this, if she were alive to see it."

"I don't know," Jake says. "I know one thing, though. She would have taken him in. She wouldn't have denied him, like you're doing."

There is quiet in the kitchen for a long while then, and that hum, that electrical voice of Jesus, seems to me to keep getting louder and louder and louder and louder and louder.

MY FATHER SAYS HE REMEMBERS being down in the well with my grandmother. He remembers the smoke and the flame and the roar of the blaze above him, and the way my grandmother stood up to her hips in well water, her blue flower-patterned dress floating around her waist. If the fire had been at any other time they surely wouldn't have made it out again, or not with as few injuries as they did. Earlier in the year — in the spring, say — and the well would have been full at twelve or fourteen feet and they would have drowned or refused to jump at all and been burned up. Another month — at the end of August — and the well would have been almost dry and my grandmother might have broken a leg. As it was, she twisted her ankle in the fall, and underneath the water it swelled and bruised and she would feel a twinge in that ankle the rest of her life when it rained, or when it was hot.

"Just the Almighty's way of reminding me," she'd say about it.

They stayed down the well for a full day and night. They listened as the fire took the house and the barn. They heard the hound stop barking. They felt the water around them get warm, and the steam start to rise as the fire swept over the top of the open well. And after it was over they heard the deep silence,

144

the steady drip-drip of water on the rocks falling into the well, looked hopefully up into white disk of daylight at the top of the well and waited for someone to come. I imagine them down there, my grandmother, bedraggled, up to her waist in cold well water, holding my father tight to her chest, the two of them looking up at the world. The vision brings me to the edge of something, some kind of knowing.

It was like they were looking out on the world, and looking in from it at the same time. It was like they stood for something that's important, that means everything to them, but I can't name or talk about or put my finger on.

WE EAT BREAKFAST TOGETHER — JAKE, Jake's dad and me. Jake's dad doesn't talk much. After breakfast, Jake tells me to go outside and play for a bit. It's sunny, and I don't need a coat, but Jake makes me wear one anyway. I hope Jake won't be long at Johnny Lang's or his dad will let me stay here while he goes to church. I am also worried, 'cause of my dream about Johnny and Jake and knowing now it was true.

Sometimes my dreams can be like that.

Once I dreamed Sammy, our dog, would get hit by a car, and he did, two days later. He wasn't hurt bad, though, except, a year later, he got shot and Jake and I buried him in the woods behind the house underneath a cross Jake built out of yellow pine he stole from the mill.

Another time I dreamed Mom would win money, and the next night she won the jackpot at bingo at the Masonic Hall. She came home with four hundred dollars. Boy, was she happy.

I tried to tell her about my dream but she looked at me funny. I could see she was scared by it, so I didn't tell her no more when I had dreams and they came true.

But there were lots of times that happened, though sometimes it was hard to tell what was gonna come true and what wasn't until after it happened.

Like I knew now Johnny had chased Jake with a gun, like in my dream last night in front of the television at Mom's house. I didn't think the part with the canoe would come true, or Wendy and baby Lucy. But I was worried because Jake thinks Johnny will be better now, and let him take the car and put down the gun. I keep thinking of my dreams and wonder if that's true.

FROM THE TIME RUTH DIED when I was five until the time of her own death when I was eleven my mother would not allow me to step foot near the river or go swimming with my friends. My father tried to talk to her. If there was adult supervision, and I was careful, he said, he saw no reason to deny me this. But my mother was adamant I would not go, and my father respected her wishes. Often kids from North River would take inner tubes up to the first bridge above our house and then come down the river all the way to Eight-Mile Bridge and the Great Falls, a five-mile trip in all, and I would stand on shore and enviously watch them go by our house laughing and waving and shouting at each other as the current carried them along. I was twelve before I went with them. I waited a full year after my mother was gone before I asked my father.

"Go," he said. "But be careful. And remember, Jacob: whatever you do, God is watching. And now your mother is watching too."

I enjoyed my time on the river.

I enjoyed drifting down it laid back on a rubber tube gently warmed by the sun and trailing my arms and legs in the cool water. My head laid back and my face turned up into the sun, eyes closed, directionless, but always moving forward. Downward. Onward. But my father's words always stayed with me too. On the tube, being carried by the current down the centre of the Memragouche, there were no trees, no houses, nothing above but sky and clouds. God and my mother could see me clearly. My sister Ruth too. It seemed more of my family was in the sky than here on Earth, and the river some kind of narrow, blue, heartbreakingly soft passage between them.

JAKE TELLS ME TO STAY away from the river, so I do. But it's hard, because Jake's house sits almost on the river and the temptation to go down to it is strong. If I lived at Jake's house I'd fish out of the living room, or go diving into the water from an upstairs window.

So what I do is I play in the barn and take rocks from the side of the road and sit on the grass and throw them in the river. I lie back and watch the white clouds sail like ships across the blue sky. I see a man and his team of oxen come by on the road and I stand out by one of the red maple trees and watch them. The man nods to me when he goes by and I nod back. The oxen are big, and red, and I see the muscles bunch under the skin in their shoulders as they walk and the way the red wooden yoke holds their heads together and the bells hung around their necks ring as they pass. They look sad, like they know where they are and what they're under. After they go up the road a bit I go out and look at the pile of oxen shit on the road, still steaming. I look at the houses up and down the road in Middlebridge. I stand in the road and look up again at the clouds and sky, at the red maples, and the oxen, disappearing around the bend in the road, their bells still ringing clear and cold in the morning.

I feel for a minute like crying for how new and shiny and clean and perfect everything is.

I SIT AT THE KITCHEN table and watch as Brian Joudrey goes by with his team of prize-winning oxen. He marches those animals up and down the road every Sunday for no good reason I can see, other than to show them off and keep them exercised for when he enters them in the North River Agricultural Exhibition at the end of September. He's won four blue ribbons running for size and form, though he always loses out to Doug Flemming from Oldsport when it comes to the Friday night ox pulls.

"That man never goes to church," my father says, staring out the window at him.

He doesn't need to, I feel like saying. He's got blue ribbons to believe in. But I don't say it. The old man doesn't take lightly to smart talk about religion.

Both of us watch as Nathan goes out and stares down at the ox shit and then stands in the middle of the road and stares up at the sky.

"He's dreamy," says my father. "Like you were at his age."

"I worry 'cause he doesn't have any friends," I say.

"He'll have even less when you take him to Halifax."

"How do you have less than none?"

"Don't get fresh. You know what I mean."

I sigh and take a sip of my coffee.

"Well," says Dad. "I should go get ready for church."

"What about Nathan? Can he stay here?"

"I'd better bring him along."

"I thought you said —"

"I know what I said. But he might set the house afire. Or go near the river. Does he have anything to wear?"

"I brought a few clothes. He could get cleaned up and I'll find him something. What'll you tell your congregation?"

"Nothing, I suppose. I'll say he's visiting. But I want you to promise me when you take that boy to Halifax you'll put him in Sunday school."

"We'll see."

"Well, go call him in to get ready. I'm running late as it is."

Dad goes off to his room and I go to the front door to call Nathan. But he is already back from the road and sitting on the stoop, playing with a stick in the dirt.

"Whatcha doing?" I ask.

"Jake," he says. "Do you think those oxen are happy?"

"Don't know," I say. "Why do you ask?"

Nathan shrugs, his back still to me as I stand in the doorway. "Just wondering."

"That's good. You'll be going to church with Dad while I'm gone to get the car, okay?"

"Okay," says Nathan.

He looks up into the sky again. I look up after him, wondering what he sees there, besides a few wispy white clouds scudding across a broad basin of blue.

MY GRANDFATHER USED TO SAY riding a log was like riding a horse.

"Both'll buck ya if ya give 'em half a chance, and neither of 'em's got any goddamned brains."

My grandfather hated horses. He wouldn't board any at the farm, though there was lots of call for that and he could've made some extra money. "Horses are the most disloyal, stubborn, deceitful creatures on Earth," he told me once when I asked him why he didn't keep any. "Most of 'em would rather kick you twice rather than look at you once, and I'll be damned if I'll have even one of 'em around to sink a hoof into me."

My problem was I loved horses. Horses seemed to me to be smart, gentle, sensitive, alert — all the things my grandfather said they weren't. I didn't like cows. They stank. Their rumps were caked in their own shit, and they were stupid. You had to be careful when you were milking them they didn't kick you. A horse kicks straight back, but a cow kicks from the side, in a kind of roundhouse. One good kick can kill you if it gets you in the head or chest. Sometimes my granddad's cows wouldn't let their calves feed, and my grandfather had to tie a rope around their necks and hold their heads off while the calf crawled under

154

to suckle. Even then they'd sometimes kick their own baby, or lie down on him.

I've never heard of a horse doing that.

MY FATHER DIDN'T TALK ABOUT Ruth, but my mother, when she was alive, did once in a while.

"She was a pretty little girl, you remember, Jacob?"

I didn't remember. Not really. But I would nod and say I did, just to make her happy.

I do remember the night Ruth drowned in the river. How the fire trucks came, and the police, and my mother in the kitchen sobbing with the women. My father on his knees on the riverbank with some Middlebridge men around him, praying. They all forgot about me. I sat on the swings and looked at the sky, wondering what all the fuss was about.

When they dragged Ruth's body from the water, my father shouted to the Lord and cried. I could hear my mother wailing inside the kitchen. I caught a glimpse of Ruth, her hair blacker and thicker now that it was wet, her dress torn and heavy with water, as the firemen carried her from the river and put her on a gurney and threw a blanket over her.

Some of the men held my father back while he screamed and fell again to his knees. He asked God how He could have done such a thing. Later, when they gave her a pill, my mother slept. My father sat at the kitchen table staring at his hands, saying nothing. They forgot to put me to bed.

I slept with my teddy on the sofa in the living room, until my father found me there in the middle of the night and made me go to my room.

They closed off Ruth's room that day. No one went into it for a year. They later made that room into a sewing room, and my mother would sometimes go into it and you could hear the sound of her electric sewing machine firing like a tiny machine gun in it.

When Mom got sick and she couldn't sleep with my dad anymore they moved her into that room, which is where she died. Then my father washed down the walls and floors and closed it off for good, though sometimes I knew he went in, in the middle of the night, and prayed.

My father thought I'd not been in that room since my mother died, when I was eleven. It was always locked and he kept the key in the right-hand drawer of the desk in his study. Once, when I was sixteen, I stole the key and went in. There was no bed anymore, but my mother's sewing machine was still there, on a table in the corner, and an old dresser with a vase of plastic flowers on it — faded purple. There was an old metal trunk of my grandfather's from when he was in the war, where my mother kept scraps of old material for her sewing.

But it was the walls I stared at.

They used to be white, but now three of them were blue. Marked up, scrawled up, with ink.

Small, cramped writing I recognized from my father's sermons he wrote in longhand and then got his secretary at the church to type out for him in the middle of the week on her Underwood.

I looked close.

In the beginning, my father had written beside the door, just below the ceiling, *was the Word, and the Word was God.*

He'd written out the Gospels on the walls.

He was still writing them out, for there was part of one wall only half filled with writing.

I left the room and put back the key and never went in there again.

"I SAY UNTO YOU," JAKE'S father says. "Love your enemies, bless them that curse you, do good to them that hate you, and pray for them which despitefully use you, and persecute you; that ye may be the children of your Father which is in heaven: for he maketh his sun to rise on the evil and on the good, and sendeth rain on the just and on the unjust."

I sit in the back of the church, watching Jake's dad on the pulpit in his suit and his hair slicked back and holding the Bible in two hands in front of his face like it was a baby. He told me to sit in the back and pay attention. I try, but people keep turning around to look at me. They whisper. And after a while I get bored with the sermon. I look out the window at the graveyard and wonder who is buried there. Is Jake's mom? His little sister?

I'm not scared by graveyards.

"Ye are the light of the world," says Jake's dad. "Neither do men light a candle, and put it under a bushel, but on a candle-stick; and it giveth light unto all that are in the house." He goes on about the salts of the earth and the poor people in spirits and other stuff and I think how it is all so much easier according to Irene, who only talks about salvation and the everlasting blood of the lamb.

After the sermon they sing songs, and the old woman next to me shows me where in the book to find them. I put a dime in the offering plate. Jake's dad gave it to me in the car on the way to church.

After it's over, Jake's dad disappears into the back and I go out on the front steps to get some sun, and there is a whole bunch of old men and women standing there.

"Where you from, sonny?" one of the old women finally asks me.

"North River," I tell her.

"You Carla Whynot's little boy?" she says.

"Yes, ma'am."

"And who would your father be?" It seems like everyone on those steps gets quiet all of a sudden, waiting for me to answer. And then I think of something real smart.

"God the father," I say. "And Jesus the son."

But instead of confusing them like I want to do the old woman smiles. "You must have some of the blood of the preacher in you," she says, and turns away to go down the stairs with her husband.

Long after everyone leaves and Jake's dad still hasn't come out of the church, I stand on the steps thinking about Jesus telling the disciples about the salt and the law.

AFTER HALF AN HOUR JAKE'S dad comes and gets me. I am nearly falling asleep in the sun. He is still dressed in his preacher clothes. "Come inside for a minute, Nathan."

I follow him out of the sun into the shadows of the church. It is cooler than when it was full of people. The sun shines through the stained glass window above the altar. It glows. In the glow, Jesus is surrounded by children.

I can read. I can read real good. *Suffer the little children to come unto me*, the words say at the bottom of the window.

I ask Jake's dad why Jesus would want the little children to suffer.

"It doesn't mean that," he says. "It means *let* the little children come unto him. 'Suffer' is another word for 'let.'"

"Then why don't he just say 'let'?" I ask.

"You shouldn't question what Jesus does or does not say," says Reverend McNeil. "It's isn't proper."

"Sorry," I say.

"Besides," says Jake's dad, "Jesus walked the Earth a long time ago, and things were said differently then."

"As long ago as Alexander?"

"Alexander the Great?" he says, looking surprised.

"That's him," I say. "As long ago as that?"

"Not quite as long," says Jake's dad. "How do you know about Alexander the Great?"

"I'm named after him," I say proudly, and I tell him all about my father giving me that name. I don't say Jake, 'cause I can tell he's like Mom and doesn't like to talk about it. When I'm done he says, "Well, Alexander the Great lived more than three hundred years before Jesus. He was a heathen."

"What's a heathen?"

"Someone who doesn't believe in God. It was okay to be a heathen before Jesus was born, because those people didn't know any better. But now is a different story. A person can go to Hell for a long time for not believing in Him after He was born." Jake's dad looks at me hard and I know what he's thinking, 'cause I remember the talk he had with Jake at breakfast.

"I believe in Jesus," I say.

"Do you?"

"Irene Lang says Jesus is a part of everything. That He's just beneath everything, like the Earth or air, something that's always there but that sometimes you don't think about or can't see. But it's holding you up and keeping you alive just the same."

"Irene Lang sounds like a wise woman."

"She also says Jesus helps those that help themselves."

"That's also true," says Jake's dad.

"Jesus is just beneath the skin," I say, thinking of Jake.

"Amen," says Jake's dad.

THE LAST MONTH BEFORE MY mother died she didn't come downstairs at all. Doctors came and went. We had to be quiet so she could sleep. At night I sometimes heard her cry out and my father would get up and go in and give her more morphine. I was not allowed to have friends over. Even in the yard I had to be quiet because the sound could carry up to her room and disturb her. I used to like throwing rocks at the power lines where the sparrows were lined up, and seeing them all fly off at once if I managed to hit the wire. I didn't stray far from home that summer, in case my mother wanted to see me, so I got pretty good at chasing off the sparrows, until my father came out and said the twang of the wire when I hit my mark was disturbing my mother and would I please stop.

"Besides," he said. "Those birds are God's blessed creatures. You have no right to disturb their rest."

Most times, that last summer, I would take a rod and go fishing in the river beside our house. You weren't allowed to fish with a reel in the river after April because you might hook a salmon, but I was too young to manage a fly rod. Normally my father wouldn't have let me fish either, but that summer he didn't care. Apparently trout weren't quite as blessed as sparrows

163

and at least I wasn't disturbing my mother. Sometimes, when being in the house got to be too much for him, he would bring a lawn chair out and sit and watch, though he had a walkie-talkie with him in case my mother needed something. She kept the other one in her room, though she hardly ever used it.

Doctor Bell told me once after my mother died she endured more pain without the use of drugs than any person he'd ever seen. She never complained. She never got mad, like sick people are sometimes supposed to do because everyone around them is healthy and they are dying. She never asked for the morphine that I remember, and so the only times my father gave her some was when she made those cries in the middle of the night.

Later I thought how much my mother must have been hurting to cry out against her will like that.

I REMEMBER JOHNNY HAS A phone.

He hates paying for it, and he rarely answers it, but he needs one in case his supplier calls on short notice and he has to make a quick pickup.

"Business expense," Johnny says about it.

I decide to give him a call, after Dad and Nathan leave for church, to see if he's come down and back to his senses. That would be a lot safer than sneaking back on his property and taking the car without talking to him. Maybe if he is all right he'll just offer it to me. I dial his number from memory in my father's kitchen. He answers after only one ring.

"What the fuck you want?" comes Johnny's voice on the line.

"Hey Johnny," I say. My palms are sweating and it feels like the phone is gonna slip right out of my hand. But my voice is steady. I keep it steady, as I sit down in the kitchen chair, the phone still to my ear.

"Hey McNeil," Johnny says. "Where are ya?"

I don't see any point in lying. He'll know where I'm at anyway. "At the old man's," I say.

"Ahuh," says Johnny. "I figured. I wasn't sure if I got you in the river. I looked around a bit, but I didn't find nothing."

"You didn't get me," I say. "I guess I got lucky."

"Lucky's the word," says Johnny. "I had you dead-to-rights, motherfucker."

"You still mad?"

"Who me?" says Johnny. "Never was mad to begin with, bub."

"You still want to kill me, then?"

"Maybe," Johnny answers. "Depends on my mood when you get here."

"But why, Johnny?" I say. "It doesn't make any sense. You'll go to jail. I'm dead. What good is that?"

Johnny doesn't say anything for a long while. Finally, just when I'm about to say something, he says, "I told ya: you've changed. Who says you get to get away, McNeil? Who says you're so much better than the rest?"

"I'm sorry, Johnny." It's all I can think of to say. I hate myself for sounding so weak. But I am doing it for Nathan.

"You coming for the car?" Johnny says finally.

"I need it," I say. "I gotta go back to work tomorrow."

"Come get it then," says Johnny. "I ain't gonna stop ya."

"You're sure?"

"I'm sure," Johnny says. "Just come get the fucking thing before I change my mind."

MY GRANDFATHER TOLD ME MY grandmother became a Christian down in that well while she waited for someone to come and rescue her from the fire. She prayed for a full day straight, with nothing to eat, her little boy crying, and standing in cold water from the waist down. They rescued her eventually, when men from the volunteer fire department came to see what was left of the house. They pulled my father out first, and then my grandmother, who fell down on her knees and started praying to God and thanking Him for saving her life and the life of her son.

For two days she and my father were put up in the Masonic Hall, where the North River Fire Department Auxiliary made up beds and cooked food for those burned out in the fire. They finally tracked my grandfather down in the logging camp up north, and brought him home. When he found my grandmother in the Masonic Hall she was kneeling beside her bed, praying. Already my grandmother had decided my father was going to be a preacher.

After they moved into the farm in Middlebridge, she made him sit down every day and learn his letters straight from the Bible. By the time he was ten he could quote that thing backwards and forwards. My grandfather complained he was living with two saints.

I know how my grandfather felt. When I was kid, whenever I did something wrong, my father would drag out sayings from the Bible and make me listen to them. It seemed like the Bible had something to say for every subject on Earth. By the time I was sixteen I was so sick of hearing it I swore I would never crack it open once I got out on my own.

My mother knew the Bible too, but she rarely quoted it.

Some people are cows, and some people are horses, and there isn't anything on God's green Earth will ever change that.

"NATHAN," JAKE'S DAD SAYS. "I want to talk to you."

We are still sitting in the front pew. We both look up at Jesus suffering the little children to come unto him. Jesus is dressed in blue, and all the little children are dressed in red and yellow and green and they look real good. Nobody looks poor in that window, 'cause their clothes are too clean and bright and full of light. I get so wrapped up in looking at all the children suffering unto Jesus I forget to answer Jake's dad.

"You hear me?" he says. "I want to talk to you."

"Yes, Mr. McNeil," I say.

"Reverend McNeil," he says.

"Reverend McNeil," I say.

"Does your mother beat you?" he says then.

Suffer the little children.

"No," I say.

"Jake says she does."

"If Jake says she does then maybe she does," I say. "But I don't remember it."

"She never hits you. Or hurts you? Or knocks you down?"

"No sir," I say. "Once I fell down and I broke my collarbone, and Jake thought she did it, but she didn't. I really fell down,

169

and Jake didn't know."

"Why would Jake tell me such a thing, then?"

"I don't know. Maybe he didn't tell you exactly."

"He told me exactly," says Mr. McNeil. "He says she beats you a lot, and that's why you're coming to live with him."

"Maybe it's true," I say. "But I don't remember it."

"Nathan," says the Reverend. "I want you to tell me the truth now. Does your mother beat you?"

Suffer the little children to come unto me, sayeth the Lord Jesus.

Dressed in purple and red and yellow and green.

IT TAKES ME ALMOST AN hour to walk from my old man's place to the River Road. I could have hitchhiked. I used to hitch that road when I was a teenager and wanted to get into town and away from my dad for a while. The one good thing about being a preacher's son is that people always pick you up. There were always people coming back from Dad's sermons in North River, because there was no Baptist church there, just United. They would pick me up on Sunday and say, "You're Reverend McNeil's boy, ain't you?"

They would talk to me about God in the car, as if because my father was a minister I wanted to be one too. I couldn't tell them that being a minister was the last thing I wanted to do with my life. I didn't know if I even believed in God. I used to believe. The last time I remember believing was before my mother died and I looked up into the stained glass window in the church during one of my father's sermons, the one that shows Jesus sitting with all the children, and I felt warm and good and safe for the first time since my mother got sick.

I thought it was God.

Later on, after my mother died, I thought it was the heat, or the way the stained glass window looked so good with the sun shining through it and all those children dressed in such bright colours.

IT ISN'T UNTIL I GET to the River Road that I remember what I am doing and, start to get worried. I keep expecting Johnny to step out from behind a tree with a gun and say, "Rejoice and tremble, McNeil," like he did in my dreams. It takes me a half hour to walk that road, though it is only a kilometre and I could have done it in ten minutes. I'm not in any hurry to get there. I keep thinking about the bruise on Nathan's rib cage, and how he looked up at me with such a trusting look on his face.

Kids got nowhere to go when their parents don't treat 'em right. They're stuck there like they're in prison, until they're eighteen or so and they can get out on their own. If I get out of this alive, I'm giving Nathan a better life.

The river flows only one way.

AFTER MY MOTHER DIED, THINGS got too quiet in our house. In the evenings my father would go into his study and work on his sermons. I would sit at the kitchen table doing my homework. I was a pretty good student, because my father made sure I did all my homework. After I was done he would check over my facts and figures and make sure everything was correct. If it wasn't, he would make me sit down again and do it until I got it right. Sometimes I sat there for three hours or more and my father stayed in his study, the two of us not saying a single word to each other. At ten o'clock my father would get up and come out into the kitchen and tell me it was time for bed. I would lie in my room and hear my father weeping to himself in what used to be his and my mother's room at the back of the house. I could picture him in there, lying face down on the bed, his face buried in his arms. That was the only time I remember feeling sorry for my father, and it was then I realized he wasn't God. He was only a preacher, a man of God, and they weren't the same thing.

IN THE CAR ON THE way back to his house, Reverend McNeil says he wouldn't mind going to see Mom for a little bit.

"What for?" I ask him.

"I want to talk to her," Jake's dad says. "I want to make sure that's she's okay with you going to Halifax with Jake. What do you think of that?"

"Can I stay in Middlebridge?" I ask him.

"I think," says Jake's dad, "it would be better if you came with me, and we talked to her together."

I don't say anything. I stare out at the river and the houses as we drive by. After a while Jake's dad turns on the radio, and we listen to gospel music. The song they are playing is "Amazing Grace." I know it, because Irene Lang sings it to me sometimes when I visit her house in the afternoons after school.

JOHNNY'S PLACE LOOKS DESERTED. The Pinto is sitting where I left it in the driveway, and the curtains in the cabin are drawn. The sun is shining through the trees and the water is rushing down over the falls. It seems so peaceful.

Except Johnny could be standing behind any one of those windows with his twelve-gauge shotgun pointed at my head and I wouldn't know it. I step into Johnny's yard and stop again, waiting for the blast. It doesn't come.

Maybe he's asleep, I think.

I take another step. And another. And I am almost to the car when I realize something.

I don't have the keys.

They're still in the pocket of my jacket, and my jacket is in Johnny's cabin on the sofa where I left it.

Part III

MY GRANDAD WAS IN THE war after he married my grand-mother. He didn't talk about it, other than to say it was a tangled-up-mess-of-goddamned misery.

He had a Nazi flag he'd taken when he marched into Bergen-Belsen with the Allied soldiers. He brought it home to burn, but didn't get around to it. My father said he found it once in the attic, and it had blood stains on it. My father also said he had seen a documentary about Bergen-Belsen on TV when he was a teenager. He knew from his mother my grandfather had been there, but when he asked about it my grandfather refused to talk.

"Consider yourself lucky," he said, "that you never have to see what I've seen. That devil you and your mother talk about ain't got nothing on what those people were up to. The day I got down back to Canada I kissed the ground outside the train station and swore I would never leave Nova Scotia again."

He didn't, either.

I didn't ask my grandfather about Bergen-Belsen.

I didn't ask him about the Nazi flag either, though my father told me about it and when I was sixteen I went up into the attic to see if I could find it.

I couldn't. Maybe he finally burned it after all.

When he died the following year his casket was draped in a Canadian flag, because he was a veteran and there were a bunch of legion members in uniform at his service. My grandfather was not buried in his uniform, though. He told my grandmother he didn't want it.

"Last thing I want," my father told me he said, "is to be reminded of that goddamned place, even after I'm dead."

My father performed his service at the Middlebridge church. My grandmother gave the eulogy, though she was seventy-five. She died herself six months later. I was a pallbearer.

The last time I saw him alive he was sick and pale in his bed. I sat with him while Nana McNeil made him some soup for supper and he told me stories about the farm. The drought in '54 and the year there were so many wireworms the potatoes came out of the ground half eaten to nothing.

We both knew he was going to die, but he didn't mention it. "You get past your father and be whatever you want to be," was one of the last things he told me. "Don't let them talk you into being a preacher. That life is fine for some, Jacob. But you and I see into things the way they don't. There's two ways of reading the world. Through a book, or through your own eyes. Ain't nothing wrong with either, but we all gotta figure out which way is good for us."

A few hours later he died, though I wasn't in the room.

A few years after I also saw a special on Bergen-Belsen and the concentration camps and for the first time saw some of what my granddad might have seen. No wonder he didn't want to talk about it.

Only once in all his long years did he mention it, when he and my father were arguing about the Bible when I was twelve in my Nana's kitchen and my grandfather said, "If it were an eye for an eye we'd go over there and turn every one of those damn Germans into lamps."

My father only shook his head. "It's not an eye for an eye. Jesus changed all that."

"He didn't change very goddamned much," said my grandfather. "Not very goddamned much at all."

"Hush now," said Nana. "We'll have none of that talk in this house."

My grandfather only mumbled under his breath, but he didn't say any more. When the two of us went into the barn after lunch to pitch hay he said to me, "Jacob? How old are you now?"

"Twelve," I said, not without pride.

"When you get to thirteen, remind me to tell you the secret of living."

"Why not tell me now?"

"I said when you're thirteen."

"I'll be thirteen in two months," I said. "It's not very far off."

"In that case," said my grandfather, stopping and leaning on his pitchfork, "I'll tell you. The secret of the world is not an eye for an eye or turn the other cheek. The secret of the world is not to get in any goddamned trouble in the first place."

With that he grunted, went back to pitching hay, and didn't speak to me for the rest of the afternoon.

WE DRIVE ALL THE WAY from Middlebridge to North River and Mom's. I don't say a word to Jake's dad. All he does is listen to the radio. I think it's a pretty bad idea to go see Mom, especially 'cause she's probably still in a mood over Jake. But I can kind of tell when it won't do any good to try and talk somebody out of something. So I stay quiet.

When we turn onto Harmony Lake Road I wish I could jump out of the car and go running back up the road to Johnny Lang's and see if I can find Jake, and the two of us could leave for Halifax right now. But the car is moving too fast and I have my seat belt on like Jake's dad told me. If I do jump out and run away he'll come after me, so there doesn't seem to be a point. But when we pull into the yard by the house, Mom doesn't come running out to see us. I sit in the car while Jake's dad undoes his seat belt and gets out.

"Are you coming, Nathan?" he says to me.

"No, sir," I say.

"You don't want to see your own mother?"

"I saw her last night," I say. I think of the place in my side where she kicked me. It still hurts this morning, and when

I looked at it before I got dressed it'd changed from blue to purple-yellow. "I'll stay here."

"You come on," says Jake's dad. "I want you to be there when I ask your mom some questions."

"What kind of questions?"

"Like if she really wants my son to be taking care of you, and all of the things Jake told me last night."

"Mom don't like questions much," I tell the Reverend. "Sometimes she gets mad when you ask them."

"Don't worry about that," he says. "She won't get mad at me. Now come on and get out of that car."

I do as Jake's dad asks, but I really don't want to. I'm afraid Mom'll make me stay with her, and not go with Jake to Halifax. We go to the door, and Jake's dad knocks. Nothing happens.

"I guess she isn't there," I say.

"Now give it a minute," Jake's dad says. He knocks again.

I am starting to think maybe we're lucky, and Mom really isn't there, when we hear her shout from inside. "Who in the fuck is it?" we hear her say.

"Carla Whynot?" says Jake's dad. There's an I-mean-what-I-say in his voice. But he isn't yelling. "It's the Reverend McNeil. Jake McNeil's father. I want to talk to you for a minute about your son."

For the longest while I just stand there, holding my breath, hoping she won't come to the door. I'm hoping the earth will open up and swallow us whole like Irene Lang says will happen on Judgment Day when Jesus comes. Anything to keep my mom from opening the door and seeing me and the Reverend McNeil standing there on the steps like little children come to suffer unto Him.

THERE ARE TWO WAYS TO get into Johnny's house. The first is by the side door into the kitchen, and the second the patio doors in the front of the house overlooking the river.

I choose the patio doors. I figure I can look in and see if Johnny is around before I go barging in looking for my jacket. I walk around the side of house carefully, ready to run in a second if I need to. I make it nearly the whole way around when a plane flies overhead. I don't know what it is at first, and it scares me. I stand at the corner of the cabin and wait for it to pass. It's a small plane, must be from the airport in Black River. I wonder as it flies overhead if they can look down through the trees and see Johnny's cabin sitting on the edge of the river. I'd give anything to be in a plane like that right now, away from all of this.

When it passes, I walk softly up the steps to the patio doors. At first, when I look in, I can't see anything. If Johnny is there, he could shoot me right through the glass. But then my eyes adjust to the gloom and I see the living room is empty. There are the sofas, but my jacket isn't on either of them. Maybe Johnny took it? And where is Charlie? Maybe the two of them have gone out? Or maybe they're asleep in the bedrooms.

I have to make a decision. Stay out, or go in.
I decide to go in.

THEY BURIED MY MOTHER ON a Wednesday. A preacher from Oldsport filled in for my father. My father wore a black suit and I wore my grey one from Sunday school. Afterwards, the parishioners came back to the house. They brought cakes and cookies and potato salad and egg sandwiches and boiled ears of corn. When they left my father wrapped it all up and put it in the fridge and he told me if I wanted anything to get it for myself.

"What about you?" I said.

"I'm going to bed," my father said, though it was only seven o'clock and still light out. "Don't forget to get up and get ready for school tomorrow."

"It's summer," I said. "There ain't no school."

"Isn't," said my father.

He went to bed and didn't get up for two days.

"WHAT'S THE MATTER," MOM SAYS when we come into the house. "Jake get tired of him already?"

"Carla Whynot?" says Jake's dad. "I'm Reverend Thomas McNeil."

"I know who you are," says Mom. "What I wanna know is what you're doing with my kid."

I can tell Mom has been drinking again. There are beer bottles lined up on the table. She must have went to the bootlegger with Jake's money 'cause the liquor store is closed on Sundays. She's standing there looking at us with a bottle in her hand. There's a cigarette burning in the ashtray. Now that we're here, Jake's dad looks like he doesn't know what to say. We wait the longest while, looking at Mom and not saying anything. Finally Mom tells him to take a seat. He doesn't.

"So," she says. "I'm asking you again, what you doing with Nathan here at this time of day?"

"Well," says Jake's dad. "Jake brought Nathan over to the house last night."

"And where is Jake now?" Mom asks.

I wait by the door, looking back and forth between Jake's

dad and Mom, who is sitting at the kitchen table. Neither of them look at me.

"He's at Johnny Lang's," Jake's dad says. "He's getting his car to drive back to Halifax."

"Ahuh," my mom says. "Figured as much."

"And he says he's taking Nathan with him. I wanted to know if you agreed to that."

"Agreed to what?" Mom says, and lights another cigarette, though there is already one on the go in the ashtray. She does that when she's drinking.

"Agreed to let Jake take your son away from you," says Jake's dad.

Mom nods. "I agreed last night," she says. "But I ain't so sure this morning."

"Jake also told me," Jake's dad says, "that he gave you some money so that he could have Nathan."

Mom shrugs. "He only gave me what's rightfully mine. I've been living here on peanuts and ashes. It's about time Jake gave me something to keep this place going."

"And are you?"

"Am I what?"

"Are you fine with Jake taking away your son?" says Jake's dad.

"Like I told you," Mom says. "That was last night."

"And this morning?"

Mom looks at me then, standing by the door, staring back at her. "I'm not sure," she says. "Maybe I should keep him around some more, until Jake gets on his feet."

Jake's dad looks over at me. "What do you think of that, Nathan?"

I don't say anything. Mom nods and takes another swig of her beer.

"It's a little early," says Jake's dad, "to be drinking, isn't it?"

"Don't you tell me what to do. I ain't no relation to you, and I don't go to that church you run either."

"I realize that," says Jake's dad, "but —"

"No buts here," says my mom. "I won't be having you or anyone else in my business. I can do what I like, Sunday morning or not."

Jake's dad sighs. "I'm worried Jake is biting off a little more than he can chew here — with Nathan. He's never taken care of a child before. By himself."

"That's what I said. He don't know from raising a kid. Kid costs a lot of money, and they need a lot of tending. How's Jake going to manage that and work a job too?"

"So you think that Jake can't take care of him?"

"I know he can't," says Mom.

"So why did you agree to let him then?"

"I told you," Mom says. "Last night I was in a different state of mind. If Jake wants Nathan he's gonna have to come back when he's got a bit more money to prove to me he can afford it."

"Afford what?"

"Afford Nathan," Mom says. "He gives me two thousand or so, and maybe I'll think about letting him take Nathan away for a while. You tell him that."

"You mean you'll sell Nathan to him?"

"She already did," I say, before I think about it. "Jake gave her money last night."

The two of them look at me. Jake's dad turns back to my mother.

"I think," he says, looking at the beer on the table, "that I'll

189

take Nathan back to Jake and he can talk to you about all this later."

"You're not taking him nowhere," my mother says. "He stays with me."

IT'S AMAZING, WHEN YOU'RE TRYING to be quiet, how much noise everything makes. I have opened Johnny's patio door a million times and it always seemed silent to me. But now suddenly it seems to rattle on its tracks when I slide it across, and the sound of the river seems louder than it ever has.

I step inside.

It smells of liquor, and joints, and cigarettes, and some other odour. The smell that's always in Johnny's house, a musty rotten smell, because he never cleans. White Shark bottles are everywhere, and an ashtray on the coffee table is overflowing with butts. A lamp beside the sofa is on, and the radio in the kitchen is playing low. Culture Club. I step farther into the room.

I see something lying between the two sofas, near the coffee table. It's Charlie Whynot. He looks asleep, passed out like he always is. Charlie can sleep anywhere when he's drunk — the floor or the sofa or sitting up in a chair. He's wearing my leather. Softly I step in between the sofas and stand beside Charlie. I reach down, easy, to check the pockets for my keys. He can keep the fucking jacket.

It's then I realize Charlie's dead. Half his head is missing. There's blood and brains all over the floor.

Sweet Jesus.
Sweet Lord Fucking Goddamned Jesus Christ.

FOR A WHILE NO ONE says a word. Mom and Jake's dad look at each other. Jake's dad takes a couple of steps back. "It was nice meeting you, Carla. Now I think I'll take Nathan back, like I said, and —"

"You're not taking him nowhere," shouts my mother. "He's mine, and not yours and not that goddamned Jake McNeil's. You hear me?"

"Yes," says Jake's dad. "But I think —"

Before he can say any more, Mom is up out of her chair and grabbing me by the arm. "You see 'im?" she says. "You see 'im? Mine, I said, and not yours or Jake's!" My mom's squeezing my arm so hard it hurts, and tugging on it too, so it feels like it's gonna pull out of its socket. I can't help it: I cry out, and Jake's dad sees my face.

"You're hurting him," he says.

"Too bad," my mother says. "I got my ways, and no white trash minister is gonna come in and tell me how to treat my kid."

Jake's dad steps towards my mom. "Let him go," he says.

"What you gonna do about it?" says my mother. She starts dragging me across the linoleum, and tries to push me into the living room. But I'm scared, and won't go. I try keeping my heels flat on the floor and she almost pushes me over. When Mom sees what I'm doing she claps me once on the side of the head and tells me to stop dragging my feet.

"Get into your room," she says. "Get into your goddamn room right now!"

And she claps me again.

"Stop that!" cries Jake's dad.

"Stop what?" my mom says. "What are you gonna do about it, Mr. Man?"

Suddenly I slip out of my mom's grip and try to turn back to Jake's dad. She hauls off and hits me harder than she has in a long while. I fall on the floor and the whole room reels and I see little yellow spots, like sparks, in front of my eyes. The next thing I know Jake's dad and she are arguing over me, with Mom screaming.

"You ain't got no right," she says. "I'll call the police, and then let's see where you'll be."

"You go ahead," says Jake's dad. "I'll tell them what's been going on here!"

"You bastard!" cries my mom. "You and that son of yours can go to fucking hell for all I care. You hear me? You miserable cock-sucking prick!"

They argue some more. Eventually Mom hits Jake's dad. He stands there and doesn't say a word. She hits him again, her hand hard across his face. He turns away from her, walks over to me, stands me up and pushes me towards the door. Mom is still screaming at us.

"Go on, Nathan," he says softly. "Go get in the car. I'll deal with your mother."

"You get back here," my mother yells at me. "You listen to

your mother, and you get back here right now!"

"Go!" he says. He really means it.

I go out to the car, open the door, and get in the front seat. I'm afraid any minute Mom will come running out and make me go back, but she doesn't. I see Jake's dad standing in the door and my mother screaming at him. He backs away from her, carefully, down the steps. She slams the door.

"Fasten your seat belt," says Jake's dad, when he gets in the car.

I could have said I told you so. But I don't. I'm just glad we got out without Mom keeping me. Before he starts the car, Jake's dad looks over at me. His hands are shaking on the steering wheel. "I'm sorry, Nathan," he says. "I'm really sorry." He starts the car and we back out and drive away.

He keeps saying he's sorry all the way up Harmony Lake Road, though I can't figure out exactly what he's sorry for.

ON THE DAY SHE DIED, I was out fishing with my rod and reel beside the river. It was a Sunday, and on Sundays when my father preached Mrs. Hunt from next door came by to watch me and my mother while he was at church. But my father must have known it was near the end, because that Sunday he didn't go and the replacement preacher from Oldsport went in his place.

"Your mother wants to see you," my father said when he came out to get me in the yard. There was nothing special in that. Most days he let me go in, unless she was in too much pain and wouldn't recognize anyone. Sometimes on the days I was to visit she cried out a lot and my father would try and give her more morphine but she wouldn't take it.

"I want to be here for my son," I heard her say to him once. "I don't want to be half in and half out of the world and not know where I am at all."

But the day he let me in, the last day she was alive, was a good day. She was sitting up in the bed, with the pillows propped up behind her. She was pale, and thin, and she hadn't eaten in days. The needles were sitting on the night table for when I left and the pain got too bad. The doctor taught Dad how to give them to her. She smiled at me. It was a horrible smile. Her face was so thin it looked like a skull, and I wanted her to stop smiling. I wanted to *scream* at her to stop smiling.

But I didn't. Because I knew my mother was in there somewhere. She was buried in there somewhere. I could see it in her eyes. Her blue eyes.

"Sit with me, Jacob," she said, and I pulled up a chair beside her bed. "Talk to me."

But I didn't know what to say.

"About what?" I said finally.

"About your day," my mother said. "About school. About whatever comes into your mind."

But nothing was in my mind except how scary my mother looked, how thin and wasted and sad. But I tried anyway, because she was my mother and I loved her. I told her about school — though it was summer and I hadn't been to school for two months — and the sun and the stars and the moon which we studied in science, and Susan Labrador, this Indian girl I had a crush on. I told her about fishing in the river and after a while I forgot she was so sick and I talked and talked and talked. After I was done she just looked at me and smiled again and this time I didn't feel like screaming at all.

"Go on now," she said. "I'm gonna try and get some sleep. I love you, Jacob."

I wanted to say I loved her back but I couldn't.

I ALWAYS WONDERED HOW MY mother could have died on such a good day, on a day when she was feeling so good.

When my old man told me she was dead and led me in to see her body one last time, I saw all the needles beside her bed were gone.

THE ONLY THING I WANT to do when I see Charlie's body is scream. I've never seen a dead body before, except my mother, and my granddad lying in his casket during his funeral, and that one glimpse of my sister when they pulled her from the river. But this is different. I vomit, and then almost break my neck trying to get out of there, but I don't get very far.

Johnny's there. He's been there all along, waiting for me.

WHEN I GROW UP I want to be a policeman. I want to help people. Sometimes I see a police car go by in North River and I think how neat it would be to drive around in one and turn on the lights when I want and hunt down people like Johnny Lang and put them in jail.

Make the world safe for people like me and Jake.

I never told anyone this in my whole life.

Not even Jake.

"YOU'RE DEAD, McNEIL," JOHNNY SAYS. "One more move and you're dead."

I stop in my tracks. Johnny tells me to turn around slowly. I do. He is sitting in a chair in the corner next to the fireplace with the gun across his lap. He's jangling the keys to the Pinto. I hadn't looked over there when I came in. It's so dark in that corner of that room I wouldn't have seen him if I did. I can't tell in the shadow, but Johnny sounds like he is smiling. I know from his voice alone that he's taken more acid. He's probably been sitting in that corner with the gun all night, waiting for me to come back.

I don't know what to say, so I just point at Charlie.

"Jesus, Johnny," I say. "You killed him."

"It was an accident," says Johnny. "It was dark. I was high. I thought it was you. He was wearing your jacket. Poor fucking Chuck."

Johnny says this with no more feeling in his voice than someone telling me what they ate for breakfast. I start to turn back towards the door.

"Don't even try it, McNeil," he says. "I got you covered."

"But why, Johnny?" I cry once more. "Why do you want to kill me?"

"I'll tell you why," Johnny says. "I'm tired of you, McNeil. You think you're better than me; I was put here to show you you ain't."

"You'll go to jail," I say.

Johnny laughs. It is a throaty, husky laugh and it makes me shiver. There's nothing human in that laugh. It's the laugh of an animal. "You think I care about jail? It's time, McNeil. Chuck's dead. You'll soon be dead. I got nothing but time."

"You're high," I say. "When you come down you'll see it was all a mistake."

Johnny doesn't answer. Instead he stands up, and steps with the gun out of the corner into the light coming in through the patio windows. He's a mess. His hair is all stuck up, and his eyes are red, and his skin white. He looks like death.

"Say your prayers, McNeil," he says, and lifts the bore of the gun up to my face.

I make a break for the door. This time Johnny gets smart. He doesn't try to get off a shot. It's a single barrel, and one shot means he'll have to stop and reload and I'll get away. I left the patio door open. Sometimes whether you get away or not comes down to something simple like whether or not you leave a patio door open.

JAKE'S DAD SAYS, "LET ME tell you a story, Nathan."

"Okay," I say. We are pulling out of Harmony Lake Road on the road to Middlebridge, and I can picture Mom back there screaming in the kitchen and throwing stuff around. I'm glad I'm with Jake's dad.

"It's a story from the Bible," he says.

"Okay," I say. I ask him if I can turn on the radio.

"No," he says. "Now listen."

"Okay," I say. "I will."

"Consider it your first lesson," says Jake's dad.

"IN THE BEGINNING, GOD CREATED the heavens and the Earth. Now the Earth was formless and empty, and the darkness was over the surface of the deep, and the spirit of God was hovering over the face of the waters.

"And God said, 'Let there be light.'

"And there was light.

"God saw that the light was good, and He separated the light from the darkness.

"God called the light day and he called the darkness night."

I RUN AWAY FROM JOHNNY'S house down the River Road as fast as I can. As fast as I ever run in my life. I don't look back to see if Johnny is coming.

You should never look back to see if anyone is coming.

That's the stupidest thing you can do.

WE GO BACK TOWARDS MIDDLEBRIDGE. I watch the river.

"The Lord God said: 'The man has now become like one of us, knowing good and evil. He must not be allowed to reach out his hand and take also from the tree of life and eat, and live forever.'"

After a while I can't see the river, so I watch the trees. We're coming up to the River Road where Johnny Lang lives.

"So the Lord God banished Adam from the garden to work the ground from which he had been taken."

I HIDE IN THE WOODS. I decide Johnny is less likely to find me there. And it's a good thing I do too, 'cause as soon as I get off the road I hear the Pinto coming down it with Johnny revving the engine and shifting like he is trying to tear the transmission out of it. I lie down flat on my stomach behind a log and try and catch my breath.

WE SEE JAKE'S CAR COME tearing out of the River Road and Jake's dad stops preaching, so I don't know what God is about to do next. The Pinto comes so fast and pulls out in front of us we nearly run into it, and Jake's dad says, "What the blazes?"

"It's Jake," I say.

"I can see that," Jake's dad says.

Jake's dad stops the car and pulls over to the side. The Pinto stops right in the middle of the road. Jake's dad gets out of the car and he is muttering something under his breath. I get out too. "What in the world is that boy up to now?" he says.

"Jake McNeil," he hollers, when no one gets out of the Pinto. "What do you think you're doing?"

Jake's dad starts walking towards the car. And the door opens and Jake's dad and I are surprised to see it's not Jake in the Pinto at all. It's Johnny Lang.

"Rejoice and tremble, Reverend," Johnny says. He's got a gun. Just like in my dreams.

I HEAR THE TIRES SCREECH when Johnny pulls out on the pavement, and then I hear another set of tires screech. I listen. I hear a voice. The voice is calling my name.

"Oh dear Jesus," I say aloud.

"PUT THE GUN DOWN, JOHNNY," says Jake's dad. "We can talk this through. Jake told me you were going through something, but we don't need to do it this way. Put it down and we can talk. You hear me?"

"I killed my father," Johnny says. "I guess I can kill McNeil's father too."

And he lifts the gun and points it at Jake's dad. But then he sees me. He moves the barrel away from Jake's dad and points it at me.

And that's when I see Jake burst out of the woods and come running up behind Johnny.

JOHNNY HAS ONLY ONE SHELL in the gun. If he shoots at me, then Dad and Nathan will have time to get away before he can reload. I run shouting out of the woods and Johnny startles and swings the gun around. I'm fifty feet from him and he still has the advantage. But all I can think is don't let it be Nathan. Don't let it be Nathan. Don't let it be Nathan.

Please God, let it be me.

IT'S LIKE EVERYTHING IS HAPPENING slow. I run towards Johnny. He lifts the gun up. Nathan is standing beside the car. Dad is running towards him too. Nathan looks like he's about to make a move.

"Don't!" I call out. "Get in the car!"

But it is too late. Johnny turns around again towards Nathan.

"Don't you fucking dare," I scream. "You fucking coward!"

More than anything in the world Johnny hates being called a coward. When he started to turn around he was smiling, but when he turns the gun back on me he isn't anymore. I'm so close now. If he hesitates one more second I'll be on him.

THE BIRDS SING IN THE trees. I hear the river far away, roaring over the falls. The sun is just above the tops of the trees, and half the road is in shadow and half of it in light. Jake's dad is running. Jake's running. Both of them are coming up on Johnny Lang. I stand there, looking back and forth between Johnny and Jake and his dad.

Then Johnny lifts the gun up to his shoulder and points it at Jake. Jake doesn't stop running.

"No, Jake!" I cry, but it's too late.

BEING SHOT IS NOTHING LIKE they say it is in books or movies. It's not a slow dying. It's a quick death. I hear the blast, and feel a pain in my chest, and then I fall back. On the road I manage to get my head turned around, and I feel like a slaughtered animal. I look over at Johnny. My father is wrestling the gun from Johnny's hands. Nathan stands there with the sun on his face. The last thing I see is the face of my son, staring at me, looking like he is about to cry.

The last thing I see is the face of my son.

I am your father, I want to say.

But I have no voice.

JOHNNY DROPS THE GUN, JUMPS back in the car, and drives away. Jake's dad has the gun. He drops it and runs to Jake who is lying back in the road with blood all over him. I stand there on the side of the road. Jake's dad is kneeling down on the side of the road holding Jake's hand and talking to him.

"Stay with me, son," he says. "Stay with me."

But Jake isn't moving. I see him squeeze his dad's hand once, and then Jake's dad shouts his name. "Stay with me!" he says, and then, "Not again. Lord. Oh dear Christ, not again!"

I REMEMBER SUMMERS, FULL OF fresh green grass and baseball and the smell of pine needles and cool river water and June bugs and badminton rackets and BB guns and the sweat of horses and fire in the fields in July and sparklers and moons and stars and indigo skies and blueberries and trout and lowing cattle and Ferris wheels and bare feet and inner tubes and swimming lessons and half-smoked cigarettes and fire hall junior dances and The Eagles and my first pint of lemon gin and corn roasts and the smell of insect repellent and hammocks and buttercups and stink bugs and swallows lined up on the telephone wires that scatter with one well-aimed rock and Popsicles and Moon Rocks and sleepovers and tents and nighthawks and the sweet smell of fresh-cut hay.

I remember so much more than I can say.

IT IS LIKE I AM floating above them, looking down on Jake, and Jake's dad crying and shouting and trying to get Jake to move and praying to Jesus to save his son. It is real peaceful. It is like I am in myself and out of myself at the same time. I float above them and watch as Jake closes his eyes for the last time and it is like everything is hanging between them. I don't cry. I know Jake's dying, but I don't cry. Jake would be real proud of me.